Mild West Mysteries:
13 Idaho Tales of Murder and Mayhem

Conda V. Douglas

Mild West Mysteries: 13 Idaho Tales of Murder and Mayhem

Copyright © 2015 by Conda V. Douglas

Cover by: Bruce Demaree

All rights reserved.

ISBN 978-1-62206-046-7

Dedication:

To my fantastic brother and fellow Idahoan, Gilbert Daladin Douglas. Thanks Gil for being the best brother ever!

CONTENTS

Acknowledgments:

To my permanent boyfriend, Bruce David Demaree, for all his support and the great cover. To my fellow author, excellent editor and critique partner, Kathy McIntosh (and thanks for the title!). And especially, as always, to my wonderful hometown of Sun Valley, Idaho, for the inspiration of my writing.

Introduction

A Brief Bit about *Mild West Mysteries* and Me

Thanks for reading *Mild West Mysteries: 13 Idaho Tales of Murder and Mayhem.*

When I began writing it was as a short story writer and short stories remain my first love today. Many of my stories (and all of my novels) take place in my beloved home state of Idaho and feature Idahoans. I'm even named after a tiny town in Idaho. Yup, I'm an Idaho gal, born, raised and fifth-generation-proud.

Sorta.

Since I grew up in the ski resort of Sun Valley, Idaho, perhaps my Idaho-ness is suspect. Sun Valley is an odd hodgepodge of playground between the rich, famous, infamous and small remote mountain Idaho townspeople. And everything, including rather ... unusual characters ... in-between, providing a sometimes overwhelming wealth of inspiration.

In these pages you'll find a couple of award winning tales, one of Idaho's Huckleberry Wars, in which bears and people fight, and sometimes both lose, a story of a garden vegetable gone deadly, a story of an Idahoan lost in the bizarre wilds of Singapore and other mild west mysteries.

Enjoy!

Conda's note:

This first story is from my Starke Dead *cozy mystery series.* Stealing Patterns *is all about my main character's, Dora's, world of jewelry design and selling, especially the hard, grinding work of selling said designs. One difficult but effective way to do that: trade shows, as is shown here—and from the point of view of one of Dora's nemeses, uh, friends, her sometime boss, Nance.*

Growing up with a jeweler father, I remember many events, all too well, much like this one, without the major crime. However, there is always much of the minor crime of stealing patterns in any trade show or conference.

Stealing Patterns

"If you're going to thieve, you'd better be a little more subtle about it," I demanded of the scruffy locked-in-fashionable young man. The only note of original style I spotted on his torn jean and faded hoodie clad body was his distinctive jewelry.

Every piece of his jewelry suite incorporated elements of a revolver. He sported the barrel on a black leather wristband and the stocks and barrels of two guns strung with more leather made a necklace. Most striking, if obviously heavy, each earlobe wore earrings made out of triple brass shell casings, no loaded bullets, cradled by a gold wire hanging low on his ears.

I could see why the young designer got invited to submit to the jury and then judged good enough to be here at Boise's very first (and maybe last, if this nonsense continued) International Idaho Jewelry Exhibition. I supposed that I should be grateful that Boise grew to the point that it could now support a major exhibition. Grateful that now I only needed to drive three hours—okay three and a half if I drove the speed limit, from my gallery in ski resort Starke Idaho, instead of the many more hours to Portland or Seattle or the two-day long trek to San Francisco. Difficult to do, when the same sneaky stealing happened here.

The thief stood three feet away from my table where my ex-employee and now temporary employee, Dora, frantically placed my presentation pieces. The object of my ire covered his cell phone, held waist high with his other hand as if I hadn't noticed. Too little, too late. Perhaps he believed I was too old, being in my fifties, to recognize what he did. Wrong.

I resisted the urge to snatch the phone away and delete the photos of my award winning designs. "At the very least, be more traditional and sketch 'em out when I'm not looking, sheesh."

At a judged jewelry exhibition like this, sure every designer studied the other award winners' designs for, ahem, inspiration. Patterns, it's all about those, we always searched for new ways to make our patterns. Or, to speak true, as any good Buddhist such as myself, Nance, we'd sometimes outright copy. Maybe even copy that bracelet—I stepped closer and loomed over my fellow thief to stop us both. I'm six foot three; I can do that so well.

Mr. Scruffy shuffled backward out of my looming, grinned and waved the cell phone. "New times, new technology, and who says I'm taking pics of your great jewelry?" He pointed with the phone at Dora. Or rather at her mid-sized cleavage, the biggest part of my short—petite—assistant and part of the reason I insisted she work the show with me.

I'd also insisted, that instead of her usual heavy cotton jeweler's apron over jeans, she wear a low-cut black velvet dress, with my signature Dog Face Mountain pins attached and my award winning platinum and sapphire necklace in pride of place centered in her cleavage. That way every customer got an eyeful of my designs, no matter where they looked and most of them looked straight at that arrowed portion of Dora.

Dora straightened and glared in the chauvinist pig's direction. Mr. Scruffy shrugged an apology and walked away. He moved to the best table in the room, next to the only glass display case, a monster at eight feet tall and five wide. The case stood next to the only unlocked single door in, affording an automatic sight direction for customers, plus lots more display.

Scruffy slouched into a chair and shared something on his phone with one of his companions, a great hulking overall clad master jeweler while I wondered why and how he got the coveted First Prize place. I mean, his dramatic stuff stood out well in the glass case, but still those pieces couldn't be worth as much as one of my necklaces—maybe a security measure?

After all, the sleepy security guard sitting in the corridor next to the door didn't look like he'd be much use, although the sizeable gun in his holster might. Plus, he might just need the weapon to keep back the sizeable crowd waiting in the corridor for the show to open. I nodded. It'd been worth the thousand dollar entry fee to get into this "invitation only juried" exhibition. The organizers obviously used that money to promote and bring in wealthy, eager customers.

"Good riddance," Dora said of the departed guy, breaking into my musings. "Another moment and I'd have gone against all my teachings and smacked the snot," she continued, just as my gaze floated to the large decorative clock above the door. Uh-oh.

Ten minutes, only ten minutes left. "Never mind him," I said as turned back to our tiny table, perched next to the other exit, a fire door leading outside.

"Darn fool judges," Dora said, interpreting my grimace as she so often did. We sometimes worked great as a team. "Give you Fifth Place will they? When they gave those jerks," she pointed at Scruffy Guy and Hulk, "First Place? No woman would ever buy those earrings. They're too heavy for a woman to wear."

I smiled at her vehemence on my behalf while I took a long, careful survey of my carefully planned display. Platinum and gold rings perched, each snug on a one finger stand in a large heart-shaped pattern on the black velvet. Diamonds and high water rubies sparkled in the settings. In the center of the ring-created heart, necklaces copied the heart form.

The longest chain enclosed a smaller chain, and one more within surrounded my best piece. A rose pin of rose colored diamonds gleamed in the center. Sure, the pin would've been bland, except for the leaf curling around one petal, a leaf picked out in emeralds.

Dora crossed her arms over her chest, obscuring my jewelry. I opened my mouth to remind her she was a walking display when she said, "A touch too sparse and cutsey-wutsey, the display, don't you think?"

She snarked about the display we planned together. Typical. When would she ever learn Right Speech? I tried to teach her all I knew, and that's extensive, about our shared Buddhist beliefs. She should be grateful. Right Thought, all the way.

Well, maybe not.

I couldn't afford to bring more. I needed to sell a few pieces before making more of my high end stock. Platinum, gold, and precious gems cost and too many too expensive pieces could sound a death knell for a jewelry business.

But did the display appear too old-fashioned, too cute? I puffed out a long, tired breath. No, no. And even if it did, the form of the display helped prevent any theft. It'd be obvious if any piece found its way off the table and into a pocket, purse, or, I'd known it to happen, mouth. Should I rethink the whole thing? In three minutes?

"What if we shift the display into concentric circles instead of the heart shape?" Dora suggested.

I agreed. "Brilliant." I reached for one of the ring stands when a screech, bang and crash made me jump and Dora scream. I whirled around to see that the glass case next to the entry had toppled over, shattered glass everywhere. Hulk jeweler stood to one side, obviously the instigator of the crash. The old security guard, on his feet, stood in front of the crowd, pressing in toward the door. Scruffy guy tore his bracelet off and had the barrel released in a second. He reached for the necklace as Hulk headed in Dora's direction, hand out.

I spotted the pattern. Hulk would grab and snatch the best pieces, starting with my necklace while his buddy completed creating the gun. Then, shoot the guard and in the resulting melee, escape out the exit. How to stop—I stared at

Scruffy, who was almost finished with putting together the gun. Next, the bullet earrings. Earrings.

In an instant, I whirled around and nodded my head toward the guy, hoping to communicate my plan to Dora. It worked. Petite Dora scuttled around Big Hulk and, with me, sprinted to Scruffy. He reared back as we arrived. Together we each reached and grabbed an earring and yanked. Hard.

"Ouch!" He cried as the wires cut through the tender earlobes.

I turned in time to see Hulk bearing down on me, when a bang resonated through the room. Plaster filtered from the ceiling, where a hole showed.

"Freeze!" I heard through the ringing of my ears. In the doorway, through the frame of the fallen case, the security guard stood, gun aimed in a two handed grip.

Dora nudged my arm and when I looked at her, held up the bloody earring. "Good thing you taught me it's all about the patterns!"

Conda's note:

This story comes from when I lived in Singapore and was a film editor in the 1970s. I may have grown up in somewhat cosmopolitan Sun Valley, Idaho, but exotic Singapore presented many challenges to an Idaho gal.

Singapore is a changed world there now, although the Raffles still exists, and I hope the parakeets as well.

Blink of an Eye

In Singapore, a day of murder resembled a monsoon day. It began bright and easy, with no hint of the storm to come. The first wisp of dark cloud appeared when I sat on my glasses. Before the day ended a storm of murder roared through my life.

I yelped when I sat on my glasses.

"Is a problem?" Anna said. On her way to the clothesline, she poised a basket of wet laundry on her plump hip.

"I took off my glasses to do hot splices," I said, "and now look." I held up the glasses, the frames twisted. "Now, I can't focus on the screen of my editing machine."

"Is okay, amah fix." Amah means maid. AmericonTran, the Boise-based company, provided me with Anna two days a week.

One of the perks they gave their contracted workers like me. All those perks and the great pay convinced me to transplant myself all the way from Boise, Idaho to Singapore. I wondered now if I made a mistake, blinded by the lure of the exotic. I wondered if I could ever see this city and its' people with any clarity.

The clothes soaked a large wet spot onto Anna's sari.

"You're getting wet," I said.

"Is okay, I leave work sari here tonight, dry tomorrow," Anna said. "I know optometrist fix your glasses quick, Missy."

"Please don't call me Missy, my name's Beth." A vestige of old Singapore: I'm Missy because I'm unmarried.

Anna beamed, showing even white teeth. A Tamil Indian, Anna stood a minute, plump five feet, an exquisite coffee colored doll in her purple sari.

"I call, glasses one hour—is okay?"

"Okay," I said. "Where's this speedy optometrist?"

"You go Raffles, you know Raffles, everybody know Raffles," she said.

* * *

I jumped on the bus to the Raffles Hotel, a tourist landmark. This early on a monsoon morning the sky shone brilliant robin's egg blue, with no hint of the storm to come. I'd never visited the Raffles, the distillation of all Singapore before. The Raffles boasted white colonnades, mahogany walls, and whirling ceiling fans.

Down the hallways offices lurk. I got lost.

I found the huge birdcage in the back courtyard by sound. A crowd of parakeets chattered in high shrill voices.

"You keep away from them birds!"

I whirled to confront a man standing before me wearing an archaic white linen suit. He glared at me, blue eyes in a once attractive face, now marked by drinker's pink.

"Don't bang on the cage," he said.

"I'd never do that."

He smiled a rogue's grin. "No, I can see you're a lady."

"They tame?" I asked.

In answer, he opened the cage door.

I held out my hand with my index finger as a perch. A blue flew out and perched on my finger.

"By God, he's never done that before," the man said.

The perky little bird chirruped. I stroked the soft feathers of his blue breast and he nibbled gently at my fingers.

The man reached out and stroked the bird's tiny head. "He's chosen you as his own." He stroked my finger. When his hand moved up to rest on my arm, I drew away.

He dropped his arm and the corners of his mouth followed. He snatched the little bird off my hand. I fled.

My last sight of the man was as he precisely poured birdseed into the feeders.

I found the optometrist at last, and while waiting for my new glasses, I window shopped. I avoided going into the shops; without my glasses the wares became mere indistinct blurs. I stepped outside the hotel onto the busy sidewalk, needing to take a break from the demanding shopkeepers, eager for the first sale of the day.

A rustling sensation crept up my back and then came a sharp tug on a lock of my hair.

"Ow!" I whirled around and confronted a Chinese boy.

"*Ang mo*," said my small tormentor. Ang mo means redheaded devil, a derogatory term for Caucasians. "So you buy." He pointed at a tiny rickety table set up on the sidewalk. People flowed around the table covered with the ubiquitous white plastic Singapore "sea lions," a male lion above and a fish with curled tail below, the symbol of Singapore.

"Great works of art," the boy said, "fine crafted in ivory."

"And I've got some great plastic antiques for you, Splices," a voice came from behind me.

I winced. Judy.

"I'm Judy, one of the oil rigger widows," she had announced the first time we met. When I told Judy I edited films for AmericonTran she dubbed me Splices.

She held her third child, a "shore leave production," nestled in a basket. She pointed with her chin at something on my sun dress. "Where'd you get the feathers?" she asked.

I brushed the tell-tale remnants off and told her of my encounter.

"You met Budgie," Judy said.

"Budgie?"

"He's crazy about those budgerigars. He lives at the Raffles and takes care of them for the hotel and—" she stopped. She stared.

I squinted. Down at the end of the corridor, I caught a flash of Anna's brilliant purple in a moving blob.

9

"Anna!" Had the amah come to make sure I found the optometrist?

The figure darted down the hallway. When I turned back, Judy too had gone.

Standing there, I realized that Budgie would make a perfect "personality" for my film. I returned to his courtyard of parakeets.

He lay in a pool of blood, his skull smashed, while his birds screamed a dirge from their cage.

* * *

"You saw Anna," George Singh, the Sikh policeman, said.

"I saw purple," I said. I took off my repaired glasses and pointed them at George. "You know how far I can see?" I tapped the edge of the desk. "Not this far."

George Singh patted at his turban secured by a tiny scimitar clasp. "Purple?"

"Anna loves purple so Anna wears purple," I said, quoting Anna's reply when I asked her why all her saris where that brilliant shade. "That's all I could see."

"Ah," George Singh said. He folded his hands over his suit vest. The chair engulfed his sparse and short body.

The Singapore police wore white gloves while directing traffic, the white glinting in the sun. No dirty hands for the Singapore police, no bribes, no missing records. Murder was rare in Singapore, and dirty.

"I suppose you want a quick arrest? No matter who's guilty?" I goaded. I wanted to ruffle the policeman's feathers, or his turban, rather.

George Singh re-tucked a fold of his turban. "We only bring her in for questioning," he said.

In Singapore, a "benevolent dictatorship," I suspected a blurring of the line between questioning and arrest.

"And she did direct you to the Raffles," he continued.

"She would not direct me to the Raffles to witness her fleeing a murder," I said.

"Yes, that is a question."

I stood up and tried to pull my sweat-soaked skirt away from my legs. A doubt in the policeman's mind about Anna's guilt was all I could do, for now. I left the police station and headed for a slice of home.

The US Club, a tiny wedge in the multi-cultured delicacy called Singapore, thundered as bowling balls rolling down lanes. I ordered a tomato beer at the bar. A concoction of half tomato juice, half American beer, passed for the Singapore version of the working man's drink. I took a couple of sips before Judy jostled my elbow as she clambered onto another bar stool.

"They've arrested Anna," she said.

I didn't correct her. I wasn't about to tell her that I had been at the police station and then spend the next hour detailing my talk with George Singh.

"The gossip on the chorus line says she killed Budgie," Judy continued. The chorus line was the daily batch of sun worshippers, rigger widows like her, who lay in sun chairs along the club's outdoor pool.

"You were at Raffles today," I said.

"Sure, shopping," Judy said. When she saw the look on my face, she snapped, "You think I did it? Why arrest Anna? Because she murdered Budgie."

"Why would she murder Budgie?"

"Oh, that's easy." Judy said. "Budgie and Anna were sleeping together."

"What? No."

Judy nodded. "It's a tradition here for amahs to sleep with their masters. And when Budgie worked for AmericonTran, he had Anna as his amah."

"I didn't know he worked for AmericonTran," I said. How well had Judy known him?

"Retired early on a pension, which he proceeded to drink. He was a professional expatriate."

"Expats, the bane of Singapore," said the oil queen behind us.

Judy spilled some of her drink.

The oil queen's husband, a vice-president at AmericonTran, had his office perched on the top of the largest

11

skyscraper in Singapore. As he lorded over the riggers, so the oil queen ruled their wives. From a distance, the oil queen looked like a plump twelve-year-old. Up close carved crevices showed around her mouth.

I sensed Judy's back go stiff as the oil queen slid onto a bar stool.

"They've made an arrest," the oil queen said. "That's Singaporean efficiency for you, not like in the States."

"That doesn't mean she's guilty," I said.

"Maybe it does," Judy said.

I looked at her and she avoided my gaze. Why were these women so eager to have the murder solved?

"Bad for AmericonTran's image," the oil queen answered my unspoken question. "Besides, they've got eyewitnesses."

Now it was my turn to avoid Judy's gaze. The chorus line would have Anna convicted and executed before nightfall.

"Anna doesn't know her place. Too friendly," said the oil queen.

"She works for you, too?" I asked. I'd never thought to ask Anna who her employers on other days than mine were.

"Yes, until today," the woman said.

"I know she's innocent," I said, "and I'm going to find out who killed Budgie." With that, I abandoned Judy and the oil queen's conversation of condemnation.

I waited at the bus stop. I had found only more questions and no answers. The temptation to head back to the comfort of my editing machine almost overwhelmed me. Film's easier than people. It can be edited.

On schedule, the monsoon clouds cauled the city in grey. The bus riders all fluttered hand held fans, providing their own air conditioning. The fans beat to the pulse of the thrumming insects. Everyone and everything waited for the storm to break.

In film, everything syncs to a subtle internal rhythm. The rhythm of Singapore, the heartbeat of this city, remained a mystery to me. And I had lost my guide, Anna.

Why was I thinking of work? Any answers would be found at the Raffles.

"What about his parakeets?" I asked the hotel manager.

He had refused my request to see Budgie's apartment, with a definite, "No. Police, only."

"Who's taking care of them?" I asked now.

In answer he handed me a tiny key.

This time, instead of their usual gregarious eruptions of movement and sound, the parakeets huddled together on their perches. Did they know their master was dead and was their fluffed up, subdued manner, mourning? Then I saw that the birds' water and food containers stood empty.

As I filled the containers, the birds chirruped encouragement. Several editions of Singapore's newspaper lay at the bottom of the cage. One corner of paper stood torn and lifted and I glimpsed something wrapped in plastic beneath.

I pulled the package from underneath the newspapers. Inside were letters. I scanned the top one through the plastic. "My husband will be out of town, no one will know. Every moment away from you is agony," it read. I pulled the letters out and fanned through them. Several different hands wrote the letters. Some read like the first, but others contained a different sort of heartfelt message: "I can get you the money soon, please, please wait before you tell him." That letter was signed Judy.

"You've found them," said Judy, from the shadows. She came out into the sunlight, carrying her child's basket.

"Yes," I said. If she killed—no, I couldn't see her carrying her infant with one hand and killing Budgie the blackmailer with the other.

She sighed and set the basket down. Within the child stirred.

"It's tough when your husband spends months on an oil rig. It was just one night. I've paid for it ever since. If only I hadn't written those letters."

"So why did you?"

"He wrote to me first, it seemed so romantic, so old-worldly, so…Singapore."

"How'd you pay him off for so long?"

"One thing about Budgie, he never got greedy. And he had other victims," she said and nodded at the letters in my hand. "Trouble is things have never been better between me and my husband. Guess I took a while to get settled in here. And now," she stopped and stared down at her child.

I sorted her letters from the others and gave them to her.

* * *

"Missy, taxi is too expensive!"

Anna and I stood on the steps of the police station. The monsoon clouds waited overhead, hanging suspended in the sky, obese actors needing a cue to pour forth their fury.

"Anna, it's going to rain any minute and I can afford a taxi. And my name's Beth. Come on." I hailed a taxi and guided her to it. Beneath my hand her arm felt made of glass.

I wanted to ask Anna about what the policeman had told me. Only, scrunched up in the corner of the taxicab seat, she reminded me of the parakeets huddled on their perches.

When I showed George Singh the letters he had asked me how I managed to find them.

"The newspaper was lifted from when the murderer removed her letters," I had said.

"Or the birds did it," he said.

"Still, it shows that someone else had a motive. So, what reason would Anna have for murder? That she used to work for the man?"

He had told me.

"Anna," I said now, "why did you send me to the optometrist in the Raffles Hotel?"

"You no like him?"

"No, he was excellent. But—"

Anna said nothing for a moment, an exhausted budgie, tired of fighting against the storm. "Okay, I tell you," she said. "I get paid a commission for the recommendations to him, and others. My American bosses, like you, they need services, they ask me. Simple, yes?"

14

Simple.

The towering skyscrapers looked dirty in the monsoon, tall priests worshipping the main god of Singapore: capitalism. What could be more natural than Anna as a shill? And did you pander to the lonely ladies of the US Club? I wanted to ask her. Was it a falling out of blackmailers?

As we pulled up to Anna's high rise home, the first big lazy drops splashed on the windshield.

"Beth, your laundry," Anna said.

"Never mind, I'll get it."

"But I hung my saris on the line. They'll run and you'll have purple underwear."

How could Anna not be innocent if she worried about such a thing now?

"I like purple underwear." Another piece of film fell into place: a sari hanging on a line, an intercut, a link between Anna and the murderer.

After dropping Anna off, I directed the taxi back to the Raffles.

The boy still displayed his wares when I arrived. Soon he'd close up shop. No one went shopping in a monsoon rain while sheets of water would chase each other down the street.

As I walked toward him, he edged into the protection of the Raffles porch. He glanced down the street, ready to run.

I sat down on the damp curb, not too near his table. After several long moments, a small body plopped down next to me. A small hand stroked the red down on my arm. I waited until he spoke first.

"It matches," he said.

"Yes," I said, and pulled at a lock of my hair. He pulled at a lock too, gently this time.

"That's because it's real, not out of a bottle," I said, wondering if he would understand what I meant.

"Real," he said.

"Yes, not like the sea lion, not pretend. Did you see an amah wearing a purple sari go into the Raffles?" I held my breath.

"Not amah."

"No?" What had his young, entrepreneurial eyes seen that my nearsighted eyes missed? All I had seen was a flash of garish color. I knew, from editing film, how easy it is to visually fool people. "What then?"

"Ang mo."

"Ang mo, like me?"

He nodded and then shook his head. "Not like you, dark hair, and little, little."

"Wearing a purple sari." I knew now.

"Lady pretend, like pretend sea lion. You buy, now?"

"Yes," I said, and tugged a lock of his hair. He giggled. I bought two sea lions, which he, grinning, wrapped in newspaper for me. As he finished the clouds burst, a sea of rain pouring down.

I huddled under the protection of the portico, shivering, trying to remember the heat of fifteen moments ago. The monsoon rain scrubbed the streets. By sunset, the rains would leave the city glistening, ready for its nightlife.

Back to the police station, I thought. Granted, all I had was a child as an eyewitness. Somehow I would convince them to investigate.

Then I remembered Roger's parakeets, caged in the open courtyard. The pounding rain might hurt them. I remembered a tarpaulin cover left in one corner of the courtyard.

The birds screeched as I walked towards their courtyard.

The cage lay knocked off its pedestal, its wire door ripped wide. Escaped parakeets fluttered about, excited with their freedom, limited by their wet wings. The rain pounded an accompaniment to their cries.

In the center of the chaos the oil queen stood. She clutched her hands at her sides. Something glinted in her right hand. Her hands, cut when she ripped the wires, dripped blood. The blood mingled with the purple dye dripping from her sari. No, Anna's sari.

"He liked to cage things," she said.

I could not see her face through the curtains of rain and the wet on my glasses. I stepped closer. "How did he cage you?"

16

"At first, it was only a little, like the others, but he knew I had more, and more to lose. When it got too hard for me to pay, he showed me how to embezzle funds from AmericonTran." She sighed and looked up.

Her eyes refused to focus on me. Her mouth hung slack, her lower teeth showing. I looked at her right hand at the blade of a knife she had used to rip open the cage.

"Not so much from AmericonTran that they'd notice. Then he wanted more. I gave him more." A muscle at the corner of her mouth twitched.

I edged away. "Anna left one of her work saris at your home." I could scream, but would anyone hear me above the thundering rain?

"We're the same size, Anna and me. I tried on the sari. It fit. That gave me the idea."

"So you came here to kill him." The last scenes dropped into place.

The rains slackened and the parakeets settled as the rain stopped. Now they perched in the trees and along the court benches, fluffing their wet feathers, heads cocked, looking like the gossiping ladies at the Club chattering over a juicy tidbit.

"Look at those birds," the oil queen said. "They're free and they don't even know it."

"You were willing to let them put Anna in a cage."

She looked at me, tears in her eyes, and I relaxed. Then her hand tightened around the knife. She lunged. I threw the package of sea lions at her head. Even plastic, the sea lions knocked her flat.

Perhaps the tears were only the rain on her face.

* * *

George Singh smoothed a hand over his wet turban. Two ambulance attendants loaded the oil queen's stretcher onto an ambulance. She said not a word. Maybe she'd said all she had to say.

I pointed at the stretcher. "What happens to her?"

"Hospital, the psychiatric ward, for observation."

Another cage. "What about charges of murder?"

"Maybe not necessary and if necessary, then we'll see."

"In other words, it'll be handled, uh, discreetly."

George Singh raised his eyebrows. "Yes, my American friend, after all, we live in Singapore."

Yes, we lived in Singapore. Evening darkened the courtyard. In the fading light, the sea lions no longer looked tacky. They changed with the blink of an eye from a tourist ploy to a proud symbol. It was time to go home and see if Anna's sari had stained my underpants purple.

I hoped so.

Conda's note:

Some of my favorite things are mystery short stories, ghost stories and stories about Starke, Idaho, my fictional town that is the setting for my cozy Starke Dead *mysteries. So here's a short story that combines all three!*

Jumping the Gun

I stare at a spot above Mallard's eyebrows till he frowns and shakes his head. That makes me shake my head, too. I watch to see if he's got it.

"Okay, you can go now," he says to the murderer. He don't got it.

Some days it ain't worth being dead. I watch my latest chance at stopping my hauntin' sashay out the door.

For a man who's supposed to be worried sick about a missing wife, he sure steps lively. I can see the youth in the set of his shoulders. I can see his wife's wealth in the expensive cut of his silk suit.

Sheriff Mallard tosses the file on top of a staggering stack.

I want to shout at him. I don't yell, 'cause he won't hear my ghost voice. Instead, I concentrate on the file folder, and shift it back down in front of him. I doubt if he'll take the hint.

I use the breeze from the open window and flip it open, more for my own curiosity.

Yep, as I suspected, I see that the killer's wife's a good decade older than he. Something's familiar about her face, too, like she's an imitation of an old friend. Must be a descendant of the original settlers.

Not that there's many of them left, these days. After the silver ore petered out and the mine closed, a lot of the old timers moved out, right then. I'd been dead a good ninety years.

Good old Starke turned into pretty much of a ghost town for decades, haunted by a few lost souls with no other place to go.

And me, the town's one ghost.

Those were lonely years, just sitting around watching people grow old and die. There wasn't any chance for me to catch a murderer and quit haunting. Worried me plenty, too. Figured I'd never get out of town.

Times change. Starke's Idaho's newfangled ski resort—fool idea if you ask me, which nobody did. Every day some rich idiot shows up wanting to break their necks on our mined-out mountain. Like that young fancy man who just strutted out of here.

Mallard stares at the file and taps his finger on the page, on the woman's age. Maybe he's taking my hint. He moves his finger up to the space where the woman's maiden name is, and he frowns. I don't keep up on the residents here like I used to, but I know her maiden name belongs to an old ranching family. Land values sure have jumped the past ten years here.

Mallard shakes his head and puts the file back.

I think about materializing and giving him a piece of my mind. He's letting a murderer walk away and seeing a ghost dressed in cowboy boots and six-guns might wake him up to that fact. Trouble is, after I materialize I always end up with a walloping headache and a powerful thirst for whiskey. Ain't hardly worth it.

Mallard turns back to his computer where he's running a check on a drug smuggler. I take a look at the pile and feel a bit mean spirited, even for a spirit. I never had such a workload. Crime sure has gained popularity in the past hundred years.

'Course we had high rollers in the old days, too. They thought they were above the law, least for a while. After I'd strung 'em up they were above the law, at least in body. Simpler in those days, none of this silly "forensic" stuff confusing the issue, and, God take me, computers.

There was just me in the old days, Starke's law and order all rolled up in one man. A portrait of me hangs behind Mallard's head. Since it wasn't taken from life, it doesn't look like me. Still it's an honor.

I like to think it's because of my hundred percent conviction record that I'm remembered. In my career of six months, I caught horse thieves, claim jumpers, and rowdy drunks, and hung two murderers. Found out later neither of 'em were guilty. I got to catch a real murderer before I can quit haunting.

And here one sauntered out after leaving a missing person's report. He figures he's taking the suspicion off himself. I expect that's for when the body shows up later, so's he can inherit her money. Hang the husband, I always say.

The phone rings. Mallard answers and listens, a big frown on his hairless face. Never did figure out why any lawman would be clean shaven and baby smooth—just gives the wrong impression. Mallard hangs up, grabs his coat and runs out the door.

I don't think he's headed for our friend's house. Probably another cocaine bust. Meanwhile our murderer is home free. Or is he?

I stare up at the portrait of me on the wall. Always bothered me that it's of the town's undertaker and he looked a great deal more like a sheriff than I ever did. I sure didn't have that full head of hair. Though after a hundred years I find it's hard remembering my looks. Yep, it's my centennial. It's getting old, being an old ghost.

I decide to do something about ending my haunting.

I'm not supposed to catch this guy my own self, just lead the living sheriff to it. But what harm would what they call a "stakeout" do? Besides, I'm the best person I know for a stakeout. I can't be spotted unless I materialize.

So I head over to the address I seen on the file form. I sorta think myself over there, sure beats walking. I used to be able to catch rides on carriages, but I've never gotten used to riding around in those automobile death boxes.

The address is an ugly mansion that looks like it's been thrown together out of discarded mining shafts. It must have cost the wife plenty. In front of the house are parked a couple of those sport car monsters, one red and one black. From the girl mess in the red one, it's hers. So where'd she run off to,

21

without her car? There's no taxi service in little old Starke. I wish Mallard was here to wonder the same thing.

As he's not, I float up the walk and in through the front door. The inside foyer is as ugly and expensive as the outside. Money makes murder.

I see a shovel propped up against the wall next to the door. Sloppy. I wonder where he buried her. In the cellar?

That's where we found old Mrs. Murgutroud buried. Hung her widower, Mr. Murgutroud, the same day. Some said I shouldn't have been so fast to hang a man over eighty. Quick justice, I called it. I found out later that he'd buried her there to avoid paying for a funeral. Too cheap to live, I figure, served the old boy right.

The husband comes down the stairs, forcing me back into this crazy present. He sure don't look like the worried sick fellow what left the office. He's changed into designer jeans and a pink silk shirt. That shirt alone might get him hung in my time.

I remember the guy's name as being Jody Farragut. What kind of a sissy name is Jody? No wonder he's turned out bad.

He's whistling. If Mallard could hear that! In his arms he carries one of those fancy leather suitcases and it's heavy by the way he's using both arms. Wonder what's in it? Where's he headed with it?

The doorbell interrupts him, one foot hanging out over the stairs. He frowns and I think he's not going to answer. Then it rings again like somebody's froze their finger to the button. Quick, he puts the case out of sight, and shovel, too, before he answers the door.

He opens the door to another reason for murder.

She's young and got a great figure, almost all of which I can see as she's only wearing a skimpy handkerchief of a top and shorts so short they might as well not exist at all. Some things have improved in this century, although I find it real difficult to concentrate now. When alive, I used to get excited at a glimpse of ankle.

"Hey, baby," she says, slipping inside like a water snake racing down the creek.

"What are you doing here?"

"Seeing you." She gives him a syrup smile. He don't smile back.

"I told you not to come around here, yet," he says. He looks past her, out the door.

"Don't be silly, nobody's seen me." She thinks maybe the smile isn't enough, so she slips her arms around him and snuggles all that glorious flesh up against him. It's enough to make me wish I had a body again.

"You know what this podunk place is like," he says, not embracing her back. "Blink at another woman when you're married and it's all over town."

"Ah, lover, I just couldn't stay away," she says, and punctuates her protest with a kiss.

He doesn't kiss back. Cold blooded murderer, sure enough, he pushes her away.

She pouts. "You got the money?" she says now, all business.

"No, not yet," he says.

"The tickets?" she says, her eyes shining with greed.

"Of course not. When would I have time to get those?" He's angry now, and she cringes away from him. I'll bet he's a woman hitter. Didn't use to hang men for that. Should have.

"But what if they find her?" she asks, real soft and quiet.

I listen close. I'd sure like to know where he put the body.

"They won't find her," he says. He looks toward where he hid the shovel.

"Why not?" she says. "Where'd you hide her?"

"Shut up," he yells. He grabs her arm, lifting her up onto her toes. She gives a little scream and I think maybe I'm about to witness another murder.

He half-pushes, half-carries her to the door saying, "I'll call you when I'm ready, until then, don't come here." He ends this with a hard shove out the door.

She stumbles and falls on the steps and before he slams the door I see her face. If there was any love between these two it's gone now.

23

He smirks at the door. Then he goes and fetches the suitcase. He opens it and I see an airplane ticket on top of stacks of money. Only one ticket, he's ditching the girlfriend.

I sure know I have got the measure of my man, now. Sleeping around, wife catches him out, wants a divorce so he kills her. Now he's lost what little nerve he had and he's bolting. If I was still sheriff he'd be kicking air by now.

He glances at his watch, frowns, and races up the stairs. Got to catch his way out of town. I follow him up to the top of the stairs and hover there.

I don't know where Mallard is, and this fool's escaping. I'm going to be haunting for another hundred years, if I don't do something quick. I get an idea.

Everything happens real quick. I wait till he comes out of the bedroom, dressed in a suit. As he reaches the first stair, I materialize right in front of him.

"You're under arrest," I shout.

I forget he can't hear me. Just after I shout, I hear the front door open. It must be the girlfriend, back for another round.

He's startled, and his foot misses the first step and down he tumbles. Good, a couple of broken bones will keep him occupied until Mallard arrives.

Only it's not the girlfriend screaming at the bottom of the stairs, it's his wife, and Mallard is with her. My murder suspect's broken a bone all right, a neck bone, from the way he's laying all twisted.

After a couple of minutes, his ghost joins me, and we both stare at his corpse. Mallard's called the ambulance and then gone to get the wife a drink. I sure could use one, too. Been way too many years and now this, my whistle's more than dry. Besides it's nonexistent.

"I thought you killed her," I say to him. I'm real disappointed.

He keeps staring at his body, stunned, or like he's figuring a way to get back inside.

"Forget it, you're as dead as I am," I say, to snap him out of it. "How come your wife ain't dead, too?"

24

He looks at me, then back to his wife, who, now that Mallard's gone out of the room, is smiling.

"I was going to kill her, you old fool," he says.

"Going to?" Now I'm feeling real confused. Same feeling I used to get often when I was alive. Sheriffing ain't easy work.

"Sure, she was coming into Boise this afternoon on a flight from San Francisco. Went shopping, you know? I was going to pick her up at the airport, kill her, bury her, and then head to Mexico. She must have caught the puddle jumper to Starke to surprise me."

"Surprise," I said. "You wanted a divorce?" Usual reason for killing a spouse, back in my day.

"No. Had a prenup, I wouldn't get a dime. I couldn't stand another day being married to the old bat."

"But the money?" I'm trying to take all this crazy fool nonsense into my old ghost brain.

"We got a joint account that I emptied this morning. What do you think I was going to live on in Mexico—dust?"

Reminds me of the second murderer I hanged. Found a fellow with a satchel full of money in a seedy hotel one day. This fellow was so poor you could see his poverty in the sorrowful droop of his ancient shiny suit.

His lady friend, the only clerk at our bank, is gone missing.

So I figured I had me a murderer with embezzled funds and since it was the weekend we had a Sunday hanging. Turned out on Monday he'd come into quick money by gambling on Friday night and sent his lady friend on a trip shopping for her wedding dress down at the state capital Boise.

When she got back, she was none too pleased, seeing as how she'd never see thirty again and he'd been her only way out of spinsterhood. Fact is, the whole prospect of spending her life as a clerk so depressed her that she used her lover's gun to shoot me. Hope it cheered her up some.

They didn't hang her for her crime; the jury seemed to believe she had just cause. Put her in jail, where she married the matron's brother. It turned out all right for her.

But I'm still dead, and a ghost to boot.

Jody tells me he's a ghost because he had every intention of killing his wife and to stop being one he's got to save somebody from being a murderer.

Seems to me we're in competition one with another, seeing as how I got to catch somebody after they do murder, not before. My fault for always jumping the gun, I guess. Jody's plenty upset about being dead.

But at least now I've got me some company.

Making It Last takes place on Harrison Boulevard, the iconic street in Boise's historic North End neighborhood. The North End was briefly my very first home. It then became my home again as an adult for fifteen fun years in the funky neighborhood, living in a 630 square foot house. Though I no longer live in that part of Boise, I'll always adore the North End.

This is one of two "holiday themed" stories. Well, sort of. Making It Last *brings new meaning to "heartwarming." And the family Thanksgiving portrayed here is a lot more dysfunctional than any family Thanksgiving I've ever attended. Hopefully you either!*

Making It Last

Ellen took the last sip of her traditional after Thanksgiving tea, made with a tea bag for the single cup, instead of the pot. It was still almost warm. A frisson of pride worked its way up her spine. She'd made it last. She could make it all last. She would.

Across from her, her nephew Albert sat slouched in her husband's old armchair, legs stretched out in front of him. In this posture, his small pooch of a belly protruded.

For a moment, Ellen worried that she'd served too much Thanksgiving dinner. Then she dismissed the worry. The Cornish game hen and potato they'd split, along with a couple of pumpkin cookies was less food than last year. Besides, she prayed it was the last year she'd have the expense of feeding Albert. And, most important, the emptier his stomach when the brandy hit it, the better.

"So what do you say, Aunt Ellen?" Albert asked, pointing at the brochures on the table of different nursing homes.

They resided in miles-away Nampa and Caldwell. Ellen's lip curled at the cheaper places, knowing her nephew picked them as the nearer to Boise, the more expensive. There was not even a single brochure from nearby Meridian. Staring at the garish, cheaply printed brochures spilling out of their plastic bag, her mouth tightened further. The filthy horrors lay, an obscenity on her antique rosewood tea table.

She'd nagged her dear late husband Henry about the expense, when he'd bought the table, thirty years ago. But being great quality, the table provided decades of beauty and service. Bless Henry. Ellen sometimes forgot that every so once in a while expense cost less, in the long run.

But not now. Not in this case. Now Ellen needed to act. She congratulated herself on having made the decision before Albert came for Thanksgiving dinner. He'd arrived with these horrible brochures, more nails in his coffin.

The brochures and bag left trails in the heavy dust from where Albert had tossed them next to his tea set. He'd set the cup and saucer down with no care for the rosewood finish.

Another, if minor, reason she'd decided on repeating what had worked before. Now, after she'd been so content for the years following Henry's death.

Boys will be boys, Ellen scolded herself, trying to shift her anger. Who grow up to be men who do exactly the same as they did when they were boys, exactly like her husband, exactly like Albert. Like uncle, like nephew. Ellen smiled at Albert, affection warming, filling and easing her damaged heart. Silly boys. Silly men. They never learned.

"I know it's difficult to choose from so many great retirement communities …" Albert said, trailing off at his fib and then rallying. "But if you choose today, you can be in your new place before Christmas."

Stupid boys. Stupid men. She should have never listened to that too-young new investment counselor. He'd promised to reduce her fees by fifty percent and he had. Sometimes she got what she paid for. Now, with her investments crashing, it was up to her to ensure the money lasted.

"Thanksgiving really isn't the time to discuss such things, Albert," she chided her nephew. If he was too upset, he might leave without drinking the brandy.

Ellen leaned forward in her chair to reach and move the tea cup and saucer away from the edge. The small shift in position caused a stitch in her heart side and she settled back with a grunt. She coughed to cover and hoped Albert hadn't heard such an unladylike noise.

He seemed not to notice. Instead he appeared to be staring at the bone china cup and saucer she perched delicately on the tiny side table. Or perhaps he saw the horrid tarnish on the antique silver teaspoon lying in the saucer, a wedding gift from Henry's side of the family. Her side would have never spent so much on a gift, no matter the occasion.

Albert looked at her. "Of course, it's the perfect time to talk about it, when else do we see each other, except the holidays?"

She wanted to say, "When you want money," but refrained.

He pointed at the tarnished spoon. "Even more so now when you're struggling with keeping up everything."

Ellen regretted having to let faithful Molly the maid go, after all those years of excellent service. (Although, Ellen recalled, Molly left with a bang of the door when Ellen had refused to pay for the last cleaning. Why should she pay for slipshod work?) She regretted she could no longer accomplish the simplest, easiest, littlest task of housework. Her mouth crimped into a wavy line. Most of all, she regretted ever having given Albert the loan for his real estate license.

He'd failed the license test. Three times. He'd never repaid a penny of the loan, much less the tiny bit of interest she'd charged. Only eight percent, compounded daily, where could he have gotten a better deal, or with his lack of credit, any deal?

Now, she needed to stretch her remaining funds even further.

Albert took a sip of his tea. He wrinkled his nose. "This slop—swill—stuff's gone cold," he said. "I'll take it into the kitchen and nuke it."

Oh good, they were that much closer to when he'd ask for the brandy. Since Henry's death, she'd refused to serve the brandy after Thanksgiving dinner, even though it had been a tradition while Henry was alive. No refusal tonight, tonight Alfred could drink all the brandy he could hold.

She sat up straighter in her plastic-covered-antique-she-found-at-a-yard-sale-a-steal-who-cares-if-it's-miserable-to-sit-in armchair. She ignored the sharp painful stab under her heart.

"Dear Bertie Boy," she put every ounce of syrup she could muster into her despised childhood name for him and was rewarded with his flinch, "I don't have a microwave, remember? I possess a perfectly good stove that does the same thing."

Albert compressed his lips in his usual reply to the familiar argument. "Yes, yes, Aunt Ellen," he said, "'Why spend money for the sake of convenience?'" he quoted her in a high, mocking tone.

Her face crumpled. She tried to force the smile back on. Although she knew how her wrinkles showed when she smiled.

When her beloved Henry mentioned plastic surgery, she'd demurred. Why mess with nature, she'd asked? When Henry turned to his younger assistant she breathed a sigh of relief and gave her used makeup and girdles to Molly, a generous tip, in her opinion. Not in Molly's. When Henry paid for the assistant's workshops in bookkeeping, well, then—with a jolt of hot agony Ellen jerked back to the present.

She shifted, hoping she wouldn't have to take one of her nitroglycerin pills. Though they didn't cost much, she didn't want to get in the habit of taking one at every little twinge. That would be foolish and spendthrift. Henry took all sorts of drugs for all sorts of conditions (including a suspicious blue pill). What good did it do him, in the end?

Ellen didn't want to take a pill in front of Albert. She knew how much the dear boy worried about her health. She had the evidence of his misplaced concern right in front of her, in the form of those horrid brochures, resting on the table, another stain.

Albert looked at her face then down at his still-full tea cup. "I apologize for that remark about convenience. It was ungracious and rude," he admitted.

She blinked.

"I know you're on a tight," here Albert showed his teeth, "budget." He set the teacup down into the saucer with a clatter.

What should she say? What would please and relax Albert, in this (she hoped) his final Thanksgiving dinner together? Ah. Of course. She knew what might work.

"Perhaps you're right," she said, "perhaps I do need more ease in my life." And she knew how to get it.

Albert leaned back in her husband's old armchair, sloshing tea over the lace antimacassar. Her mother's. From the Depression. The real one. The great one. When people scoffed and said there could never be another, Ellen always pointed out that's what they said about the Great War.

"What, you're agreeing with me?" Albert's eyebrows rose almost where his hairline used to be, back when he was young and handsome and charming.

Same as dear Henry, who'd swept Ellen off her feet many decades ago, with expensive roses and perfume and at last an enormous five carat diamond ring. The same ring now remained on her wedding finger. She would have put it into the safe deposit box after Henry passed to keep it forever, but she couldn't get it off her now always swollen finger.

"Yes, of course, I am, you're such a clever boy," Ellen said. She gazed around her dusty front room. "But you know it's so difficult for me to even imagine leaving all this luxury."

With the curtains drawn to protect the furniture from sun fading and one low watt lamp on, the room appeared as it had before Ellen's husband passed away. Rich, luxurious, expensive, to match the outside of the mansion sitting on Boise's Harrison Boulevard, in the oldest neighborhood, the North End, once the one and only upscale neighborhood.

Ellen's mansion, built by a nineteenth century Boise mayor of brick, would stand forever, never changing, the mortgage paid off. However, property taxes rose, ballooning upward in the always uber-chic neighborhood.

All those years ago, after hubby died, she'd gone over the finances and realized that on her meager widow's pension of a few thousand a month, she'd have to be careful, attentive and parsimonious. She'd created a time capsule to last the rest of her life, her, she hoped, long, long life.

"Luxury?" Albert said, bringing her back to the present.

He stared down at her beloved, wonderful Aubusson carpet where she'd easily covered the worn-through spots with inexpensive throw rugs. It'd last.

"What luxury? Where?" he asked.

She opened her arms in a wide, expansive gesture to the glorious, expensive room.

Albert gazed up to the cream colored, so classic, ceiling. He reached up towards a long, large cobweb hanging from the room's main light, a carved milk glass globe from the magnificent Art Deco era. "This place is a fire trap."

She dropped her arms. How could Albert say such a cruel thing?

"I'm surprised you haven't croaked in a blaze."

For a second, Ellen wondered if he'd considered setting fire to her home, with her trapped within. Staring at his weak chin and drinker's-vein-dappled cheeks, she realized he'd never possess the guts to do such a thing. She was about to tell him so, when he said, "But if you sell now, while it's still not a gutted shell—"

"Nonsense, nothing a little dusting wouldn't fix," Ellen snapped, and grimaced at her harsh tone. At least she hadn't blurted out about his cowardice.

Albert stared in her direction. "Have you been drinking?" he asked. "I mean, I know it's good for the heart—"

"No, that's your expensive addiction," Ellen said. She bit her lower lip. She knew her last words, her reminder of how she disapproved of his drinking, might keep Albert from drinking in front of her.

"I wouldn't need to drink if you'd only give me the money—listen to reason," Albert said.

"Good save, nephew, at least of words," Ellen knew she shouldn't have said that either. "I'm sorry. You know how I worry about money."

"You wouldn't have to be so tight-fist—I mean so worried," Albert said, another save, "if you'd just accept the change in your life and move on to the next stage." He sighed. "You could spend some money, live a little." He set down the tea cup with a cracking clunk. "Sorry, Aunt Ellen. Really."

Now it was Ellen's turn to sigh. "I'll glue it like the others—"

"I'm sorry my plans haven't worked out," Albert continued as if she hadn't spoken. "If they had, I'd have the money to help you, and there'd be no question of it running out."

He sounded so bereft that for a moment Ellen wavered on her own plans.

Then he smiled at her, his best insincere salesman grin, all lies, and said, "Assisted living is my best idea yet. You buy the condo and your worries and mine are over."

She stared at his hopeful face, with the ravages of years of indulgence cutting deep discontented lines, and she wondered at how much he resembled Henry.

"So if I move out—" Ellen began. Her heart gave an unwelcome jump in her chest. Never happen, she reassured her delicate organ. She'd remain in her beautiful, hard won mansion forever, with the only way she'd leave would be feet first.

She sniffed to smell again the faint always comforting aroma of her husband's pipe tobacco, still present even after fifteen years. So much better than the presence of the man himself, she mused, so less expensive to deal with, easy, simple, uncomplicated.

"Move out, move on, move forward," Albert said.

"Forward? How do you move forward in a nursing home?" Ellen demanded. "The only forward in those places is into the grave."

At the word "grave" Ellen thought she spotted a small smile on Albert's face. There were advantages to never spending the money on eyeglasses. Without such crippling assistance, her eyes still could spot the smallest telling detail.

Then he shook his head. "Not a nursing home. Assisted living is completely different." Albert spread his hands wide in imprecation. She always hated it when he begged. "Which with your heart condition, you need." He picked up the top brochure on the pile. He thrust it toward her. "Come on, Aunt Ellen, you have to be reasonable."

Insistent. Pushy. Just the same as his uncle, whenever Henry wanted something.

"Consider the alternative," Albert continued, "and nothing and no one lasts forever."

She stared at Albert's stained, frayed and tattered shirt cuff. He wore one of her husband's favorite silk shirts, highest quality. Ruined, trashed simply because Albert insisted on paying for dry cleaning instead of using those lovely, delightful inexpensive dryer sheets at home.

Her nostrils spread wide. "If you'd taken care of that shirt, it would still be as good as new."

Albert's lower lip protruded. "And it still wouldn't fit me." He forced his mouth into a smile-like grimace. "Aunt Ellen, please, if you would only look at—" He flipped a hand toward the brochures, creating a small dusty breeze.

She turned her head away.

He dropped the brochure back onto the table. "I'm only thinking of your welfare," he said in a low sad voice.

A doubt whispered in her mind. Perhaps he did care about her. She shook her head. No, he was only thinking of his own good. What she planned was for his own good, as well. He'd hate living poor. So would she. She knew how he'd spend the money. It'd never last.

First, however, she needed to convince him otherwise. Needed him to believe she'd leave her home, her life's blood. "I know, dear heart," she said. "I understand."

Albert's small, beady eyes narrowed in suspicion. His eyes almost disappeared into his bottom eyelids, into his drinker's fat pouches beneath.

She pressed her hand over her aching heart. "Really. I need to think of my own welfare." And she was.

No change in Albert's expression.

"And to seal the deal," Ellen said, with a bright thought, "let's have our traditional Thanksgiving brandy?"

Albert frowned. "Aunt Ellen, it's been years since we drank Uncle Henry's brandy, for any occasion."

Ellen winced. Of course that was true, but she'd counted on Albert's alcoholism to make him not care. "It'll be all the better for having been saved."

Albert glanced sidelong at the thousand-dollar-brandy-bottle on the bookcase. "Saved—that's right. You never want to use the last of anything."

"But things are changing—let's start with the brandy—an old tradition becoming a new one?" Ellen hoped her words hadn't sounded desperate.

Albert's frown deepened, turning his face into a twin of his uncle's. "The last of anything, much less the much contested brandy." He gave another quick look at the bottle.

Ellen groaned inside at the memory of one of the few true fights she and her Henry had waged over his purchase of that bottle. Sometimes sacrifices must be made, sometimes you have to spend in order to save, she reprimanded herself now. She'd thought the same while pouring the powder into the brandy.

She straightened, tightening her resolve around her aching heart. "But after all, dear boy," she said, "it is Thanksgiving."

Albert looked again at the bottle and this time his gaze held. He licked his lips. So close to success … inspiration hit Ellen again.

"Why don't you take Henry's snifter?" she asked. Henry's snifter—big enough to drown in, to die in. "I only want a tiny taste to sip and roll over my tongue. You know, to make it last."

That did it. Albert jumped up so fast he knocked his teacup and saucer off the table.

Ellen didn't look at what she knew had to be the carnage of her special china. She'd glue the pieces together later, after the ambulance left. It'd be fine.

Albert poured all of the brandy into the snifter. He forgot to pour Ellen's bit, as she had hoped and half-known he would. He took a huge gulp. He coughed.

Ellen's body jerked, trying to get her to jump to her feet. She forced her body to relax and settle. Surely, Henry's prescription pills wouldn't work that fast?

"Mmm," he said. He smacked his liverish lips. "It's aged well. Much sharper." He took another large swallow, almost draining the glass. He sprawled back into Henry's armchair, finished the brandy, and used the empty glass to gesture at the brochure. "Now, about the condo, it's perfect for you, but you need to move—"

She leaned back into her armchair with a crackle of old plastic. "It doesn't matter if it's the Taj Mahal, and they charge enough for that tiny condo it might as well be, I hate the very thought of leaving my wonderful home."

"Home? You mean this mouldering mausoleum?" Albert flung his ill-fitting-silk-shirted-clad free arm wide and gestured to take in her front room.

"Put Henry's glass down," Ellen ordered. He'd already cost her too much this visit. "I won't have you destroying another heirloom and wasting my money."

"Your money?" Albert slammed the glass on the table. It survived.

Ellen suppressed a giggle. Unlike Henry, or Albert would.

"Don't you mean Uncle Henry's money? And this tomb?" Albert continued before Ellen could protest. His florid drinker's face grew redder. "A memorial to my uncle, who, let's face it, Aunt Ellen, you always despised?"

"I never—I loved your uncle." A hard pulse started in Ellen's temples.

Albert gave a short, hard bark of a laugh. The alcohol and drug cocktail must have gone to his brain and loosened his tongue.

"You loved his money. And what it could buy." Albert raised his chin towards the room.

"That's not true—I—" She grabbed her bottle of nitroglycerin tablets. She let go. No, not yet. It'd all be over in a few moments. Then, in the new silence, her heart would settle and quiet.

Any second now Albert would collapse. Heart attack brought on by his lifestyle, they'd say. Ironic, they'd say, when it's his aunt with the bad heart.

"Not as much as you, nephew," she said when she could speak. "You've spent it fast enough." She jutted her chin toward the brochures on the table. "If we're facing facts, Albert, I know you want me out of here so you can sell my home. How much is this place worth?" Even in a rundown condition, she knew the place would be worth plenty. Housing prices in the ultra-chic North End, especially the iconic Harrison Boulevard, seemed to skyrocket daily.

"Aunt Ellen—" Albert's face glowed a deep, dark red. He leaned forward in his chair. His hands twisted in front of him, the knuckles white.

"The problem with you, Albert, is you've never known how to make anything last." Ellen used her cane to knock the brochures to the floor. "I'll not let you force me out. I'm here until I die."

Albert stood. His shoulders slumped. "I believe you, Aunt Ellen."

"Which will be a long time from now," she added, hands clasped to fallen bosom.

"No, it's only true you'll be here until you die," Albert said. He pulled the plastic bag off the table. "But it won't be a long time." He stepped around the rosewood table toward her.

"Albert?" A pain started behind Ellen's eyes. "Nephew?"

He grimaced, mouth turned down in regret. "It was you who taught me the necessity of stretching the money out. The condo was my last and final offer. There's only one other option. With the life insurance policy I took out—"

"You wasted money on—" Ellen couldn't complete the sentence, for the pain now jabbed, hot stabs of agony.

"Not a waste and cheap at the price," Albert said. His mouth quirked into a twisted smile. "With the insurance money and the money from the sale of this house and furnishings and without your expenses ... there'll be plenty for me for a long, long, time."

Ellen leaned back into her armchair. Her breath came in short gasps. She regretted her earlier thrift with her nitro pills. She remembered her mother always saying to her, "Penny wise, pound foolish, that's you." Ellen never listened. She never understood. Now, at last, she did.

Albert smoothed out the plastic bag. "All I have to do is cut off your air—"

"But—but—they'll know I was suffocated." Agony built in Ellen's chest. It won't be like your death, she tried to add, but couldn't find enough oxygen in her lungs to speak.

"Not if your heart stops first."

"Please…" was all she could manage.

"This is going to take a while," Albert said, holding the plastic bag stretched wide in both hands, "I'll make it last." He brought the bag down over her face.

She clawed at the plastic, but he held it fast.

As the last few beats of her heart faltered, Ellen reflected that she should have used one of her own prescriptions to poison Albert. Henry's pills had been long, long expired.

Useless. But she hadn't been able to bring herself to throw his prescriptions away. And she was so proud to have found a use for them, long after she'd used them to poison Henry. The same use for Albert, it possessed a wonderful, thrifty sort of symmetry.

Or so she had believed.

As the last of her life slipped away, she thought all she ever wanted was to make it all last till the end.

And she had.

Conda's note:

One of the traditions in Idaho is every year, in certain parts of the state, we have Huckleberry Wars. Huckleberries are a member of the blueberry family, smaller and sweeter and much prized. People squabble over huckleberry patches growing in the woods. Sometimes, bears, also aficionados of the berries, join in.

The bears always win, unless of course, it's bear hunting season.

Mama Chin's Last Great Bear Hunt

I stared upward at the great bulk of the bear where it laid on the deer trail, a furry lump half hidden beneath a huckleberry bush. Myriad questions flooded my mind as I studied the odd tableau.

Next to the bear, Dora stood, arrayed in an oversized bright orange hunting vest that clashed with her red hair. I'd known Dora since she could only ask me for a cinnamon roll in baby talk. With her hands over her mouth, she gazed wide eyed at the bear, as if she'd never seen a dead animal before. Which I believed must be impossible. In the mountains surrounding our little town of Starke, Idaho, almost everyone, with the possible exception of Dora, our one and only Buddhist, often hunted during the season.

However, the fall hunting season started tomorrow.

Dora shivered in her lightweight shell and hugged it tight around her. I scrunched my shoulders in sympathy. What was Dora doing out here in the cold woods? I shook my head. Trust Dora to be inappropriately dressed for the fall day, having perhaps done something inappropriate for a Buddhist, with an inappropriately dead bear.

"Dora?" I called out. I used my best "calm but firm" voice. Dora sometimes resembled a perpetually startled squirrel. I thought Buddhism, with its tenets of meditation and

39

acceptance, would quiet a person down some. Didn't seem to work with Dora.

Her head jerked up and she let out a tiny "eep," followed by, "It's Mama Chin." Again with surprise, as if everyone didn't know I snuck out to go hunting the day before the season. Most recent years, that didn't signify anything illegal, as I was only pretending to hunt, pretending to kill my annual bear and foregoing the skinning, butchering, tanning the hide and rendering the fat to fill my dozen Thanksgiving turkey fryers. It's more work than it sounds.

Dora continued to stare at me with that odd look. Did she believe she knew the dead bear in a previous incarnation?

"That's right, it's me, good old Mama Chin." I tried to modulate my voice away from its usual sharp-as-knives tone. I didn't suffer fools, ever, and most people were darn fools. But Dora wasn't a fool, only foolish with a too tender heart.

Keeping my 30.06 rifle broken open and pointed down at the ground, I strode up the steep trail. My calves throbbed with every powerful step. I cursed my lack of preparation for my annual fake bear hunt. Only this year, I wasn't faking the hunt. This year, I hunted a dumpster diver bear, a bear who'd made the mistake of coming into town and diving *my* dumpster.

This year, I'd figured I'd been busy enough at my Mama Chin's Save On Café to stay in shape. I'd figured wrong. But no way would I huff and puff and maybe groan in front of Dora. I had a reputation, despite my short stature, for being tough to bag a bear just for the fat. Since my Chinese immigrant five generation Idaho family has plenty to be thankful for, the turkeys are free of charge and all you can eat.

To my gratification, the turkey fry up has become a tradition in Starke, with most of town turning out and turning it into a huge pot luck. I provide my signature turkeys; everyone else provides the side dishes and desserts. Then we all eat way too much, but I figure that's traditional.

Now Dora took a couple of steps away from the dead bear. She glanced up the trail as if she needed an escape route, but from what or whom I didn't know. It couldn't be me.

"Did you kill her?" Dora asked me. She spoke through chattering teeth, the clicks of her teeth distorting her words.

I frowned. "How do you know it's a she?" I reached Dora and the bear. I stood with one leg forward, bracing myself. I panted, a little, not so much that I figured Dora would notice. Or so I hoped.

Dora pointed downward and I got my first good look at the bear.

I gasped, the icy air cutting into the back of my throat. I tasted all the little deaths of fall, the tang of fallen leaves, the smoke from a fireplace somewhere near, and perhaps this new awful death.

Not a bear. The too-white face barely peeking above the fur coat told me that and told me who.

A person.

An annoying, difficult and newbie of a couple of years to our town. Still, a human being.

Arianne.

Arianne wore her signature mink fur coat, an old tatty thing. She shed fur like some gigantic ancient cat. I always tortured her for coming into to my café wearing the huge coat, always told her I was afraid the health inspector would close me down for having giant rats. She never got my humor. She never got much of anything about us longtime residents of Starke.

I stepped forward and reached toward Arianne. "You're sure she's gone? You checked?" I snapped at Dora, and then regretted my harsh, scolding tone.

But Dora appeared to remember that was my way. "Of course I did," she snarled right back at me. "It's obvious."

"What's obvious?" I asked. I looked closer and then saw what she meant. Arianne's eyes stood frozen open, with one eye resting on, no *in*, the dirt. The taste of a partially digested cinnamon roll from breakfast flooded my mouth. I swallowed hard.

"Did you shoot her?" Dora's ridiculous question provided a welcome distraction from the sight. She looked back down at the bear-like form and I knew what she thought. She thought Mama Chin, me myself, had attempted to get her annual bear and shot fur-dressed Arianne by mistake.

No one knew that I'd given up bear hunting a few years ago. Used to get me a bear each fall, then I got to feeling sorry for the bears and for my 55-year-old knees.

Add to that, the fat's too saturated for our modern cholesterol-laden hearts. Also, no one noticed the switch out from bear lard to good old virgin olive oil for the turkey fryers. Or if they did, they didn't say a word. They wouldn't dare. I've been known to ban people from the Save On, more than once. It's my restaurant, and my say.

But I figured I needed to keep up a pretense of my yearly bear hunt. Turned out, my wandering around the woods for a few days became a welcome break from work, a mini-vacation. Then I'd go home and photoshop my older more wrinkled face onto an old photo of me with one of my dead bears, a bear which had been in that state for years.

Not this year. This year I hunted for real and hunted one specific bear, my dumpster diver. Although I'd never caught sight of the beast, I could tell from the trash scattered around my bin that a bear used my trash as a buffet. And I knew that meant the bear had become a threat not just to my café's leftovers, but to Starke residents. A bear that far into town was a bear without fear of humans. In Starke, we took care of our own and it was my responsibility to remove the threat.

"You can tell me if you accidentally killed her. These things happen. Not that it isn't still a bad action, bad karma, but understandable."

Dora's flood of words pulled me out of my bear musings.

I lowered my eyebrows and glared at Dora. She flinched. "I never shoot uphill," I said. "No hunter does, you know that." I shifted my gaze to Arianne. "Although, I gotta say, she does make an excellent beary target in that coat."

The wind ruffled the mink fur, making it appear that Arianne stirred, perhaps objecting to my personifying her as bear-like. But in many ways, with her stubborn, aggressive and successful business tactics, she was.

I looked down at Arianne, wondering why the woman was out here, dressed to die. I wasn't the only hunter who snuck out the day before hunting season opened. Then I spotted the telltale bucket of huckleberries tucked under the huckleberry bush. Arianne must have been huckleberry hunting, as must have Dora, both trying to get the prized berries before the bears did.

Darn fool Arianne. She always insisted that as an Eastern Seaboarder she could show us small town Idaho hicksters and hucksters how to run our businesses and lives. That is, if'n we could get those potatoes wedged in our ears out long enough to understand. That meant she never listened to our advice.

Or if she did, she only heard what she wanted to hear, such as when I told her last night, "Huckleberry pies sell great. There's patches of huckleberries all over beside the trails." But apparently she never heard my saying, "Make sure when you go out to pick 'em you wear bright colors, hunter's orange preferably." Not dress up in imitation of a game animal.

"I know no hunter shoots toward a ridge," Dora said, her voice clear and hot. Maybe her anger warmed her up some, got rid of her shivers. "It's a great way to kill somebody coming over that ridge. But that's the direction I came from and I didn't see a soul the whole way. So when you got excited at seeing the bear and shot uphill—"

I held up one hand in a stop gesture. "Whoa, Dora. I don't get that excited. And I haven't shot at anything anywhere today."

"But then how—" Dora seemed reluctant to let go of her scenario of me killing Arianne. That was our Dora, once she got hold of some idea, she hardly never let go, no matter how wrong-headed that idea was. Good thing she'd gotten a hold of Buddhism—I shuddered to think if she gone all weird cult instead.

"You've taken a jump and run off with a ridiculous idea, as usual."

Dora frowned, her face saying she suspected I just didn't want to own up to shooting Arianne.

I sighed at looked down at the fallen woman. "Listen to me, Dora." As if she would. "We don't even got any idea how long ago Arianne was shot."

Dora chewed her lower lip. "Couldn't have been days. I saw her last night."

"Me too."

Dora's chewing increased. She might eat her lower lip if she didn't ease up. "But—"

Something that I should have thought of earlier flashed into my mind. "Did you hear a shot?" I tried to appeal to Dora's common sense—I knew it existed in her somewhere. "I didn't hear a shot. So if she was shot, it must have happened right after dawn."

Dora gasped. "Then she might have been killed on purpose. Oh no, that means somebody finally got too fed up and murdered her."

I sighed. My attempt to find sense in Dora had failed, not for the first time. Granted, she appeared shook up and shocked by the death—me too. Maybe neither of us thought straight right now. "No, it only means that she may not be shot. She may have had a massive heart attack or something." Arianne might be competition, but she always was first in line at my Thanksgiving Turkey Feast.

For illustration, I pointed down at Arianne's body. Dora nodded. We both knew that Arianne gained enough weight to fill out that coat to bursting in the months after she opened her restaurant in Starke. Probably from eating her own delicious creations as well as my once-yearly turkey. I'd eaten at her place a few times to check out the competition and been appalled at how great the food was. Too much competition, for my taste, but that's how it goes.

Dora reached toward Arianne. "Let's find out."

"Ah, ah, ah," I said.

Dora pulled her hand back. She knew what I meant, but didn't know or trust what I'd do if she didn't obey. Good. She still bought into my "tough old Mama Chin" persona.

Or so I believed until she put that hand on her hip and said, "Why not? Afraid you'll faint?"

I gritted my teeth together. "No, because if someone did shoot her and shoot her on purpose then we'll be destroying evidence."

Dora put her fist to her mouth. I agreed with the sentiment she expressed in that gesture.

"I'm calling Sheriff Mallard." I pulled out my cell phone. No bars. Drat.

"No bars, I already checked." Dora *could* be sensible sometimes.

I sighed. "Okay, I'll stay with Arianne and you walk into town—"

Dora tucked her chin. "I'm not walking by myself."

I growled deep in my throat, bear-like. Dora didn't flinch. "Whyever not?" I demanded.

Dora snorted. "We don't know what happened to Arianne. Same thing might happen to me."

A vision of a crazed hunter rampaging through the woods blasting away at orange-vested and brilliant red-haired Dora made me smile. Then I remembered that it might be murder.

"Let's go." Dora started off down the trail.

I shook my head. "Wait. I can't go. We can't leave her here alone."

Dora stopped and turned to frown at me. "Why not? It's not like she'll notice and be upset."

"Because we take care of our own and there's a bear around and bears are scavengers and they're not particular about what kind of dead meat they eat."

Dora went white and I regretted my words. I took a deep breath and smelled the smoke of someone's fireplace. Oh dear, why had I forgotten? It must have been the sight of Arianne that knocked it right out of my head. Course, that family never did stand out much, real reclusive even before the dad took off.

"We'll go together to the Bristols'," I said. The Bristols lived out of town and a short distance from this ridge. It must be the smoke from their fireplace I smelled.

Dora's mouth opened in a round "O." "Oh yeah, they're just a bit aways and they're bound to have a landline or a satellite dish out here."

45

"Even so, we need to hurry." Now that I'd mentioned it and thought on it no telling where that bear might be.

* * *

Teenage Paul Bristol stood and peered at us through a 5-inch crack in the warped front door. I worked real hard not to stare at the angry zit sitting right above the eyebrow of Paul's one eye peeking through the gap. His eye watered from staring at us wide-eyed.

"Come on, Paul, let us in," Dora said, and pushed on the weathered door. That's our Dora, barreling in without a thought of how people living out in the woods might react. Here in the remote reaches of Idaho, it'd be how *armed* people might react. Here in hunting-wise Idaho, it's rare to be unarmed. Here in Idaho, it paid to remember that. Ask Arianne.

Through the widening crack, I could see Paul push back with one skinny arm. He must be at the stage where he'd shot up but not filled out, all sticks wired together. I sighed and put one hand on Dora's shoulder. "Dora, enough." She knew to stop. "Paul, we don't need to come in, we just need you to call Sheriff Mallard and tell him there's been an accident."

"Or a mur—" Dora started to say when I smacked her on the shoulder. No sense upsetting an already twitchy teenager.

Paul opened the door a little wider. "We don't got a phone."

"You don't have—" Dora opened her mouth again. I squeezed her shoulder again. She shut her mouth again. Good Dora.

I pointed at the ubiquitous old beat up Ford truck that sat to one side of the cabin, standard issue for anyone living in the Idaho Mountains. "How about you drive down to Starke then?"

Paul opened the door wider and leaned out to look at the truck. His forehead wrinkled as if he'd never seen the family vehicle before. Behind him, I could see a ways into the cabin to where a couple of dirty feet protruded over the end of a ragged sofa.

Another body? I surely hoped not. Bad enough to have one.

Then the feet twitched and the sofa body snored, a dainty, feminine sound that made me think it must be Paul's mom, sleeping it off again. Ever since Daddy Bristol took off, Mommy Bristol alleviated her grief with alcohol therapy.

I snorted at my own foolishness. Arianne must of knocked me off my common sense, not an easy thing to do.

Paul must have caught my looky-loos, 'cause he stepped out onto the cabin's porch and shut the door. "I don't know how to drive yet."

"Then give me the keys." There went Dora again, just as I remembered seeing Paul roaming around town on his bicycle, but never seeing the truck with either his mom or him driving. Heck, for all Dora and I knew, the truck couldn't be driven anymore. Out of gas or broken. Or both.

Paul's expression of a bear caught in the crosshairs of a rifle, knowing his time was up, confirmed my suspicions.

Dora reached out for the keys. I grabbed Dora's arm. "Nope, it's better we stay here and get back to the body."

"What? Why?"

"We found her, so we're witnesses at best and suspects at worst and shouldn't go off running to town."

At "suspects" Paul shifted from foot to foot, that skinny bear caught in the crosshairs about to bolt.

"I didn't—" Dora said and before she could say something that'd mean we'd both be walking to town I hustled her off the porch.

I looked over my shoulder and pointed at Paul, standing frozen. "You head down on that bicycle of yours and get Sheriff Mallard up here pronto," I ordered.

Paul nodded, obviously relieved to know what to do.

"Wait—what—" Dora dug in her well-worn hiking boot heels.

"Back to the body," I commanded.

* * *

"Was it an accident or did you mean to kill her or was it in the heat of the moment?" Dora asked me.

I stared at Dora, unable to think of a snappy comeback. Then I snatched the cinnamon roll plate away from her reaching fingers and held it out to Sheriff Mallard instead. He grabbed the biggest and gooiest before he said, "Good question."

Now it was turn to stare at Mallard. I swear I didn't know where that man put all those cinnamon rolls of mine he gobbled down daily. He remained the Skinny Sheriff of Starke. I kept my eyes on him until sweat broke out all over his face, despite the coolness in my closed café.

Dora chewed her lower lip instead of my signature cinnamon rolls. "It's okay, I understand, you can tell us, Mama Chin." Dora's voice sounded soft and low, as if she approached a living wild animal, a crabby mama bear perhaps.

"Let's see if I've got this straight," I said. "We spent hours waiting and talking and waiting up on that deer trail whilst you," I pointed at Mallard, "and those Staties took care of Arianne. Then you," I pointed at Dora, "suggested we come to my café because we were all starving."

Dora nodded and reached for another cinnamon roll. I smacked her hand away.

"And you still have the gall to eat my cinnamon rolls when you've accused me of murder?"

Dora compressed her cinnamon roll bereft lips. "You had reason to want Arianne dead."

Mallard stuffed a huge bite of roll into his mouth and nodded.

I found myself nodding too. Dora's accusation rang true enough. Arianne moved into town and opened up her own combo restaurant/gift shop/convenience store. One stop shopping in a town the size of Starke meant that for the first couple of years after she opened that's where everyone shopped. Even though Starke was Idaho's newest ski resort and so we now had tourists, still it cut deep into my profit margin. Some days I even ended up tossing a few stale cinnamon rolls out. Before Arianne, that'd never happened.

48

My nod stopped. I did some lip compressing of my own. "You had reasons too, Dora."

Dora co-owned and operated her aunt's gift shop, Mad Maddie's Marvels. I knew she'd also seen sales plummet.

She fingered her Ohm pin, a fused glass symbol of her faith that she always wore, this time on the outside of her orange jacket. "I'm a Buddhist," she replied, as if that expunged her from any possibility of suspicion. Knowing Dora, and Dora's heart, maybe it did.

I only wished she could see past my grumbly and crumbly exterior to my heart. I grunted. "Her restaurant shut down, you bet I'd like that. Maybe her run out of town, okay, maybe. She sure annoyed me, what with her 'this is how to do business' snootiness. But I never wanted Arianne dead."

"But you were the last person seen with her, last night," Mallard said, through a last mouthful of roll.

"That you know of," Dora said.

That was our Dora, first she accuses me then she defends me. This time, when she reached for a roll I let her.

"We talked about how her business has slacked off—"

Dora grinned. "About time the 'new' wore off."

"Yeah I felt that way too, but I figured she'd been in Starke long enough to be one of us. We take care of our own. So I suggested—" I stopped right before I told Dora that it was my idea for Arianne to go huckleberry picking. If she didn't suspect me before, she'd suspect me now.

She guessed anyway. "So you suggested adding huckleberry desserts to her menu, right? So you knew exactly where Arianne—"

I held up my hand in a stop talking now gesture. "There's more than one huckleberry patch around here, Dora."

"Yeah, but this one's the closest to town."

That's why I figured the bear would be there. Two-stop breakfast shopping, the dumpster first and then the huckleberries for dessert—and with the bear so full and focused on the berries, the poor thing would never know the bullet that hit him. And die happy.

"And when did you ever know Arianne to not take the easiest way?" Dora asked.

I didn't have any instances. I held out my hands to Mallard, wrists close together.

Sheriff Mallard ignored my gesture, grabbed another roll and leaned back in his chair. "Trouble is, you're not the only one with motive in this town, and so far, we got no proof of anything."

"So I'll just stay under suspicion?" I hated that idea. Bad for business.

"And others," Mallard said, looking at Dora.

Dora choked on her roll. "Me? You can't—"

"For now."

* * *

"I got him, I got him," Tony crowed. He stood next to the tail gate of his Ford truck, a newer but still beat up, model than the Bristol's. He smoothed his luxuriant moustache with one hand while with the other he pointed at the truck bed.

I stood with the rest of the group gathered around the truck. Although most of the others inched away from me, the murder suspect, save for loyal and also-suspect Dora. Arianne's autopsy showed she'd been shot. I'd turned over my guns, as had a number of hunters, but no luck—and as Dora pointed out, everybody in Idaho had "family" guns and nobody registered great-grandpa's pistol. So suspect I remained.

A bear's bristly black snout stuck out on the tail gate.

"I got that dumpster diver," Tony clarified something that didn't need clarification. Starke's main construction foreman stood tall and broad chested, almost bear-big, glorying in his moment.

I stepped up close to the truck and got a good look at another kind of suspect. Right off, I wondered if that bear could be my dumpster diver. He looked far too skinny to be a bear who'd been helping himself to a trash smorgasbord.

"How much?" I asked, pointing at the bear.

Tony stared down at his trophy. "I'm not selling my bear. I'm keeping it."

I sighed. Great at construction, sometimes a little slow on the uptake or down low about other things, our Tony. "And what are you going to do with it?"

Tony looked blank.

"Do you know how to skin it to keep the pelt? Do you know how to render the fat—" I stopped at the thought that, with my friend and customer attrition I might not need any fat because I might not have any takers at this year's Thanksgiving. "—and preserve the meat?" I soldiered on, pushing aside thoughts of twenty-five uneaten turkeys. "And then tan the skin—"

With each of my sentences, Tony's face drooped.

I sighed. "Look," I said, "I'll do all that and send the pelt off to be made into a rug and give you that rug for payment, all right?"

Tony, now grinning, nodded.

After I cooked up the bear meat, I knew it couldn't be the diver. Bear meat takes on the subtle flavoring of what the bear has been eating. This bear tasted of sage and huckleberries, delicious, but not my tossed-out-cinnamon-roll flavor I'd expected.

I considered the bear stew in front of me. I huffed. Figured it'd fall to me to get that darn fool bear that kept sneaking around so quiet I never heard—

Quiet? Bears didn't know from quiet. They created a symphony of crashing trash cans when they dived.

That meant it couldn't be a bear. Then what ...? I leaned back in my chair as a couple of pieces tumbled together. Then I knew what I needed to do.

* * *

"It's okay, Paul." I pitched my voice low and easy, like I was trying to get close to a deer for one of my nature shots.

Paul jerked away from the trash can. In one hand he clutched my bait, a fresh bag of my cinnamon rolls. "I'm not stealing. It's trash."

I reached out and placed a hand on his shoulder. His too-skinny-mom's-a-drunk-and-can't-take-care-of-her-son shoulder. "I know. Just as I know you shot Arianne thinking she was a bear."

Under my hand, his shoulders hitched. "I didn't mean to. I really did think I was shooting a bear. I didn't know what to do." He gave a single, smothered sob.

"It's okay. I know what to do." I patted his back and added, "Come on, let's get you some milk to go with those cinnamon rolls."

Turned out, the judge ruled it an accidental shooting—dang straight as that was what it was. He only sentenced Paul to community service, a class in hunting etiquette, and after Paul's mom went into a program, gave him to me to foster. Turned out, Paul proved invaluable in helping with the biggest Thanksgiving Day Turkey Fry Day I'd ever had. Turned out, people did notice the difference between bear fat and olive oil. Turned out, when I mentioned this Turkey Day would be my last hurrah frying with bear fat ... all that was left of forty turkeys was a few well-gnawed bones.

Now Paul, who's filling out fast, sleeps in my back room, sweeps up and saves his salary for a new truck. And eats up all my leftovers. And I do mean *all* the leftovers.

Here in Starke, we take care of our own.

Conda's note:

Another holiday story, this one inspired by hair. As a woman with naturally curly hair that turns into a puff ball when it grows past a few inches, I've always been jealous of women with long, straight hair. This story grew out of those feelings—and one bizarre Halloween when I wore a wig and horrified everyone.

Boise's Harrison Boulevard, mentioned previously, is famous both for the elaborate Halloween decorations (think bales of hay decorated with full size lit-up skeletons fencing an enormous blow up black cat) and the generous treats (think full size candy bars) that the occupants provide every year.

Appearance is Everything

All that hair made Robert realize how he could kill his wife on Halloween night, get away with it, and keep the money and his girlfriend.

"I'm sorry," he apologized to the tiny woman with the straight black hair that hung to her knees. "I didn't mean to startle you. I thought you were Bitty." He'd hollered "Bitty" at the woman when he'd spotted her standing at the back of the line. "Because of your hair," he said, as if that explained everything. For him, it did.

The wide-eyed woman raised a hand to her hair, palm out, as if protecting the effusive flood of black.

"My wife has the same long hair." Robert put down his personal-all-for-him bucket of fried chicken and added, "Let me pay for your meal." When the woman smiled and nodded, he grinned back at her, overjoyed at the image lurking in his mind of his wife dead.

"It'll work," Robert promised his girlfriend, Sandy, later at dinner at her place.

She shook her head as she placed the chicken salad, with free range chicken from the Boise Co-op, and little chicken in much salad, in front of him.

"I mistook a stranger for my wife and I've been married to the old bitty biddy for twenty years." His stomach growled. Robert looked down at his plate and remembered he'd been so excited that he'd forgotten his bucket of chicken at the take-out. Amazing, he thought as he patted the extra fifty pounds of padding around his middle. He dug in, for once not caring that he ate something green.

"All you saw was all that hair," Sandy said. "That doesn't matter—"

"What matters is that I made the mistake," Robert said through a mouthful of crunchy green masquerading as food. "And I see Bitty every day." He shuddered and shoveled more salad into his mouth, now ravenous. Everything about his wife made the empty space in his belly bigger.

Fifty pounds ago, that hadn't been true. When he first met Bitty, he found her name charming and appropriate for her minute stature, her mimicking of Cher's long-ago black hair and hairstyle beautiful, and her class-awareness, well, classy. It hadn't hurt that her father, Bitty's one remaining relative, owned a major computer company in mini-Silicon-Valley Boise.

"Any dessert?" Robert asked now, as he gulped the last of the too-small serving.

"But, Robert," Sandy said as she placed a bowl of fruit compote, no added sugar, in front of him, "I can't imagine that somebody won't notice."

"Who?" Robert answered. "You know that appearances are everything with Bitty. And she only makes the one at our annual Halloween party."

The October 31st holiday remained a traditional big deal in Boise, a safe enough city for children to go door-to-door. The adults celebrated as much as the kids, with large parties. None as elaborate or grand as Bitty's.

Robert's stomach growled at the remembered image of Bitty at last year's event, still squeezed into her revealing Cher costume. She seemed not to notice how the plunging neckline and slit high skirt revealed only wrinkled flesh.

Once his wife had been a young Bitty, now she was an old one. It had taken ten years of marriage for Robert to acknowledge that Bitty's classiness was only extreme snobbery. That Bitty's longterm worship of Cher was only misplaced narcissism. And that her name was only an excuse for her to never grow up.

Robert blamed Bitty's father, who'd taken one look at fiancé Robert and created an unbreakable trust for his "Tiny Treasure," another name for Itty-Bitty. Now, with doting dad long dead, and twenty years into a miserable marriage, Robert knew his only options were to kill Bitty or eat himself to death.

Robert took a big bite of the compote and almost spat it out. It burned into the back of his throat. Sandy, his health-fanatic girlfriend, had baked it with too much healthy cinnamon, to reduce his boiling high blood pressure. Sandy was the same size as Bitty, but there the resemblance ended. Sandy, with her short, sporty, curly red hair, adored Robert, adored cooking and adored new experiences.

Unfortunately, Sandy's job as an exercise instructor only made enough for her to live on. Robert, who'd never worked, didn't want to start at forty-four.

Robert looked at Sandy's frowning-in-doubt face and forced himself to swallow. "This is perfect timing."

Sandy looked blank. It was a common look with her, but understandable, with Robert's obtuse comment.

"We follow our Halloween party with our annual European trip, remember?" Robert explained. He put his spoon down. The idea of traveling for three months again during Europe's worse weather and with Bitty as she dragged him through the tourist traps of the continent—blood thundered in his ears.

Always before, he'd comforted himself by consuming mass quantities of the various cuisines of Europe. Before, he hadn't had Sandy in his life, or such high blood pressure. He didn't think he could make it through three cold and dreary months this time.

"What do you mean?" Sandy asked.

Robert sighed and reflected, not for the first time, that Sandy did share a certain dimness with his wife.

"You're the same size as Bitty," he explained. "I find a wig that matches her hair. After the Halloween party, we kill Bitty—"

Sandy gave a little squeak of dismay. Adorable. Not at all like the piggy squealing Bitty always indulged in.

"Yes, but it needs to be done," Robert continued. "And done the night before we go to the Bahamas." No more freezing his generous buns off in Europe, Robert vowed.

"The islands? Us? Together?" In an instant turnaround, Sandy clapped her hands.

"Our honeymoon. Three months later we come back, you wearing the wig …" He paused at the sight of her grim face.

She ran her fingers through her curls. Women and their hair, he'd never understand it. He resisted the urge to touch his own balding head.

"It won't be forever," Robert explained, in a patient voice he remembered using with Bitty, years ago. "You don't have to wear the wig in the islands. And after six months or so, we can say you cut your hair to donate it to those cancer patients and decided to get it dyed and permed."

Sandy nodded then clapped a hand over her mouth as if she might become sick. "What about Bitty's—um—leftovers?"

"You mean her body? Have you forgotten her one hobby? Her dirt?"

Bitty loved making dirt. She composted. Everything from the kitchen and the lawn went into an enormous, steaming pile. A tender mistress of compost, she tended the mound, stroked it, spoke to it like a lover. She even planned their European vacation around when the muck needed to "rest." She produced fabulous dirt.

She never did much with the dirt except for a little desultory gardening, a couple of tomato plants and way too many zucchinis. Robert wondered how anyone could live in Boise and not know that one zucchini plant could feed a neighborhood.

Dear god, how Robert hated zucchini, unless Sandy made her fat free zucchini pie, of course.

"It's only right that Bitty should be laid to rest where she can contribute to what she loved best," Robert concluded.

Sandy nodded.

The biggest problem Robert found was finding the wig. He didn't want to be anywhere he might be recognized as he and Bitty often patronized the same Boise costume shops, or remembered for buying an odd item for a guy. So he limited his search to the smaller stores in Nampa and Caldwell, small satellite cities of Boise's. Yet, even here, he got lucky.

Two days before Halloween, just as he was about to give up, he discovered a costume shop in Caldwell that not only had the wig, but was about to go out of business. He got the wig, on sale, and paid cash to a harried clerk swarmed with customers searching for last minute deals.

Robert's last evening with Bitty proceeded beautifully. She glowed at their usual party, tossing her long black signature hair every few moments. While she glowed, she drank. And drank. Robert added two strong sleeping pills to her last drink as they were saying farewell to the last of the guests. Bitty slumped to the floor seconds after Robert closed the door. An unconscious Bitty proved easy to smother.

That he'd smuggled Sandy into the house early that day confirmed Robert's luck. After chain sawing Bitty into itty-bitty bits, Robert found himself exhausted and with his blood pressure slamming a pulse in his ears. Still, it took him over an hour to convince Sandy she had to be the one to "compost" Bitty.

"Life as always, remember," he kept telling her, "Mrs. Browning," the standard old biddy of a nosy neighbor, "will be watching."

The old woman always watched the compost pile out her back window, even during the winter months, as if she suspected the dirt to be complicit in a crime. Who knew? This time, she was right.

Sandy, after a series of *icks*, and throwing up three times, wore the wig and dug into the compost pile to distribute Bitty's parts.

No one saw Robert and Sandy leave by taxi in the pre-dawn hours. He and Sandy boarded their flight, right on time.

The one glitch in Robert's and Sandy's three-month "honeymoon" was that Robert had to buy a new wardrobe. Twice. Instead of eating his way through Europe, he made love all over the Bahamas. Sandy also insisted on walking everywhere and swimming and snorkeling. Not enough sex or not enough activity and she'd sulk. Adorable. Sorta. By the time Robert returned home, he'd dropped his fifty pounds and his blood pressure to normal.

The first day home, Robert handed Sandy her wig and said, "Time to turn the compost pile."

Sandy's lower lip protruded. Robert hadn't seen that lip for a while. Somehow her lip didn't look quite as cute as it had before he'd murdered Bitty.

"You've got to do what Bitty would have done," Robert insisted. "At least for a while."

With ill grace, Sandy snatched the wig, smashed it on, and slammed outside.

Robert watched her forking the compost pile and considered how fortunate it was that Sandy adored traveling. Lots of things could happen on a trip. In a year's time, surely all the female DNA in the house would be Sandy's. Good for confirmation that Bitty had died an accidental death.

As he watched, three policemen approached Sandy. One took hold of her pitchfork and another took hold of her arm.

Robert's blood pressure rose to its highest ever. He stepped outside. "Excuse me, officers," he called out as he trotted toward them, "what are you doing with my wife?"

"She's not your wife," one of the police officers said. "Or at least you're not her husband."

"What do you mean?" Robert asked.

Sandy sobbed.

More police officers, CSI by their equipment, arrived. One started to gently shift the compost pile.

"Did you really think you'd get away with killing your husband?" the first policeman asked Sandy.

"Killing? I'm standing right here," Robert said.

"You were seen burying him," the man continued.

The CSI uncovered a white bone. It looked human. Maybe because it was human.

"Or at least you were seen burying several suspicious bundles," the officer continued.

"By—?" Robert started to ask, but realized the answer. He glared up at the face half-hidden in the window.

"Mrs. Snoopy Old Lady didn't think a thing about it until you returned." The police officer pointed at Robert. "But this skinny guy doesn't even look like your husband, lady. Once she got a look at him, she called us."

The CSI held up a long hank of dirty black hair.

Sandy pulled away from the other policeman's grasp and buried her face in her hands. As Sandy's wig slipped to one side, Robert reflected that Bitty was right:

Appearance is everything.

Conda's note:

As told in the previous story, Boise, Idaho is a perfect place for growing some produce. Top amongst these vegetables is the zucchini. Sometimes backyard garden newcomers to the city don't know about this vegetable's overenthusiasm and plant several zucchinis. This leads to the crime of neighborhood zucchini drive-bys, when large paper bags full of the vegetable are flung at doorsteps. That crime wave is the inspiration for this story featuring more of my characters from my cozy mystery Starke Dead *series and set in that mountain town.*

We Boiseans make excellent zucchini bread. And zucchini succotash. And zucchini pickles. And …

Squashed

I squeezed my eyes shut and opened them again. Didn't help. The sight of Dave remained. Oh, excuse me, not Dave but *Eagle Claw*, as he insisted being called, lay splayed out and too still in the dirt between a row of corn and one of overgrown squash.

A watermelon-sized zucchini lay smashed over Dave's face, with string goo packed with enormous seeds trailing from the squash down to the ground. Indents on the rounded dome of the enormous squash and the rounded impressions of knees to either side of his chest showed how someone had sat on him and pressed the zucchini down until Dave suffocated.

His hands clutched the smashed edges of the squash and one hand held a scrap of cloth as well. Without conscious thought, I knelt down and wriggled the piece loose from his tight grasp and beheld a scrap of lace. I recognized the lace pattern as one of Mrs. McGarrity's tatted creations.

I curled the lace into my fist and swallowed back the squash-flavored bile that crept up my throat. I disliked the man for good reason, but he didn't deserve such an ignominious death by overgrown vegetable.

A quavering familiar voice behind me asked, "Timmy, what have you done?"

I stumbled to my feet and whirled around to see Dora, the questioner, and Julie, Dave's current girlfriend, standing a couple of feet away. Julie clutched a smaller but still large zucchini, this one whole, while Dora held a zucchini cheese casserole clutched tight to her chest, the cheese dripping down her jeweler's apron. I almost didn't recognize Julie. She'd thinned from a size 20 down to a size 10, almost cutting herself in half. Ugh, another bad image. Almost as bad as how this must look to the two women.

"Running Bear, not Timmy," I said automatically. Force of habit from when I first opened my store, Mocs N' More a couple of years ago.

Even though I could only claim one great-grandmother as a Shoshone-Bannock, my family's moccasin-making tradition made me claim my Native American heritage. The main contention between me and Dave was his assertion of his own three-quarters Cherokee for his store and his insisting on my removing my Native American designation from everything in my store. He reveled in calling me Thin Blood Timmy.

"I've known you as Timmy O'Reilly ever since kindergarten, and that's what I'm calling you," Dora said, with hints of her stubborn, obstreperous Aunt Maddie in her words. "Now answer the question." More hints of Maddie.

"I just got here," I protested. I pointed at my own dropped bag filled with zucchini as proof. I'd planned to open the bag and use the zucchinis inside as salvos toward Dave's head, in another act of aggression in our annual zucchini war. Every year, in Starke, this little Idaho town, people grew zucchinis. Every year, people grew way too many zucchinis. Every year, Dave grew the most, because, as he always said, "It's a true Native American food." Then he'd drive by drop off grocery bags stuffed with squash to everyone, including me. I despise zucchini.

"You mean you got here before the both of us, Running Bear, and killed my boyfriend," Julie piped up, pulling me back into my current predicament with her voice as thin as the rest of her. At my glower, she ducked behind Dora and cowered, her protecting squash still pressed against her well-tucked in shirt into her Dockers. The better to show off her new waist, I supposed. No elastic-waist-mom-jeans for Julie anymore.

"Wait a minute, let's not jump to conclusions, here," Dora said, in a complete turnaround from her earlier accusation, in her usual ADD-Dora style. Or maybe her style should be called Creative Dora, for she made gorgeous jewelry—and appreciated my beaded wall hangings. "Maybe Timmy is here just like us," she nodded at Julie, "me to deliver a thank you casserole and you to pick up another zucchini for your diet."

Zucchini would make a great diet for me. I'd rather eat dirt. I smiled my thanks at Dora.

Julie must have taken the smile to include her, for she said, "But Dave—Eagle Claw—always said, 'There's only room for one Idaho Native American in Starke and that's me.' And I know he was taking away business from your store."

"Not only my store, and he did other crime, too," I protested. Everyone knew that he took advantage of the other artists around town, taking eighty percent of the profit when he sold their art on commission in his store. Mrs. McGarrity in particular, with her tatted lace creations—I thought of the lace still clutched in my hand. "He set himself up to be … squashed, one way or another."

Dora winced and stared at Dave's face covering. Julie's eyes teared up. I regretted my choice of words. Before I could apologize, Dora's gaze flipped to over my shoulder and I heard Sheriff Mallard say, "Yes, but whoever did the squashing—deed had to have been a big person, or at least heavy."

I sighed. Yeah, I'm both. With my stocky bottom heavy build, I'm more bear than running. Sheriff Mallard came up and took my arm, with a light touch, but firm enough that he could hold on if I tried to take up the first part of my name. Figured I'd be the main suspect.

"Hold on, Mallard, we don't even know how old Eagle Claw here died, for sure," Dora said.

I smiled my thanks at her for speaking up for my possible innocence. Then she added, "Sure, it looks bad and Julie and I got here and found Timmy crouched over the body—" she stopped and compressed her lips. Too late.

Mallard's hand tightened on my arm. I could feel the slickness of his always-sweaty hand and resisted yanking my arm away. The sheriff was famed for being able to sweat out a uniform in the middle of a snowstorm. The pressure on my arm eased as Mallard said, "You're right, Dora."

"I am?" Dora squeaked out the words. "About which part?"

Oh, my dear friend, Dora, always was going a touch too far, the signature sign of an artistic temperament.

"About the part that we don't know what Dave died of," I provided and added, "or even when, or maybe even where."

Mallard dropped my arm. "Sorry, Timmy."

"Running Bear."

He ignored my correction. "But you've got to admit, you've got motive and maybe means."

As I could think of no good or honest answer to that, I stayed silent. Great-Grandma always said, "Sometimes it's better to just shut up." Wise Indian woman.

* * *

Dora and I stood behind the crime scene "Do Not Cross" yellow tape and watched Sheriff Mallard and the Staties go about their work. A sobbing Julie had been escorted by Doc Byrne to his car. After Doc Byrne cleaned Dave up some, she'd make an informal identification so that the family could be notified and then go to Starke's, our tiny town's tiny police station. Mallard ordered Dora and me to stay put behind the crime scene tape until he "could take us in for questioning," he'd said, all official sheriff of Starke, Idaho.

Dora picked at the remnants of her cheese zucchini casserole on her apron. "I'm betting this will be harder to get off than my casting wax," she complained. The casserole, along with my bag of zucchini and Julie's mondo-zucchini, had all been confiscated as "evidence." Evidence of what, I didn't know, but good riddance to the squash overload.

"We've got bigger problems than your laundry," I said.

She looked up at that and sniffed in my direction. "Seems to me it might be you who has the bigger problem."

I sniffed right back at her, smelling the rank deep stench of rotting zucchini. Dave, as always, had overplanted. His garden took up the better part of an acre, so to give Dave a break, it might be easy to do, especially when one zucchini plant could feed a family of ten, twelve, fourteen … many.

"I'm not the only suspect," I told Dora. "Look what I found in Dave's hand." I pulled out the scrap of lace.

Dora gasped. "She couldn't, she wouldn't—"

"Mrs. McGarrity," I said, "might and she certainly could." Mrs. McGarrity, the heaviest of Starke's Widows Brigade, a group who took it upon themselves to be the professional busybodies of Starke, weighed in at three hundred plus pounds. She'd started tatting lace when she'd been a new thin bride— and then added lace panels to her clothing as she expanded, then started making custom clothing for others and then she started tatting lace hearts and other designs for jewelry, earrings and such.

The woman was obsessed with her craft. Then I remembered my own late night, oh heck, all nighters, working over my beaded creations, my own artistic mania, and smiled.

"What are you smiling at?" Dora demanded. "That Mrs. McGarrity is also a suspect?" I shook my head. "No, no. She's not a suspect until I give this—" I held out the lace "—to Mallard. But I'm going to ask her about it first." The old woman deserved at least a heads up, murderer or no.

I turned to go, when Dora said, "But Mallard said to stay—"

"That's why you stay here and if he notices I'm gone tell him I needed to … get something to eat or go to the bathroom or something. Stall him."

Dora looked dubious, granted she often looked that way, but before she could protest, I took off.

* * *

65

"What do you mean I killed that evil little man?" Widow McGarrity loomed over me, and boy, could she loom. I didn't know if it was her height at 5'9" or her generous girth, or both, but the widow didn't need any assistance in intimidation. She wore one of her own tatted lace creations, a dark grey dress she'd covered with layer upon layer of lace till the cloth below disappeared. She resembled nothing so much as a large roiling storm cloud, about to burst.

From years of knowing the woman, I knew that the best way to stop her thundering was by meeting it head on and never flinch. She'd never struck like lightning and killed, unless she'd murdered Dave, which I doubted. "I never said any of that, even about Dave being an evil little man."

Mrs. McGarrity huffed.

"Even though I agree with you about that last part."

That got the widow to quirk a smile and hold up her ginormous teapot, covered in a lacy tea cozy, making it even larger. "More tea?" She poured as she asked, into what must be a 16 ounce tea mug, with its own smaller version of lace cozy.

"Uh, thanks," I managed to say, even as the thirty-two ounces of the two previous cups sloshed in my stomach, along with Mrs. McGarrity's fabulous (and zucchini free) banana nut bread.

I took another thick slice to soak up some of the tea and give me time to think of how to accuse—ask—broach the subject of the piece of lace I'd found at the crime scene. Even my opening gambit: "Dave's dead, murdered and you and me are suspects," had made Mrs. McGarrity puff up, her lace dress rustling in outrage.

As I chewed, I gazed around at the widow's front-for-best room at the oversized furniture that crowded every inch. Tatted lace antimacassars covered every chair and the sofa, overflowing the arms and backs down to the floor. Yup, Mrs. McGarrity was a woman obsessed—or maybe only a woman who loved to always go big and generous.

My artist's eye caught the fine detail, hearts in a ring pattern repeated over and over, on the doily my arm rested on. I swallowed and leaned forward to study the lace pattern, completely different from the lace piece in my pocket. Gazing around, I realized that every lace piece was a different pattern, each unique and distinctive. If that was so for all of the Widow McGarrity's creations, then she'd know where—

I yanked the lace scrap out of my pocket and held it up. Mrs. McGarrity's eyes crossed as she tried to focus on her handiwork.

"Where did you get that?" she demanded.

"Never mind that." I didn't dare tell her where, that'd set off another round of "don't you dare accuse me."

I flapped the lace. "Just tell me what this came from."

She snatched it out of my hand and ran her fingers over the pattern. "Let me think ... I do so much tatting ... too much really ..."

At least Mrs. McGarrity knew about her tatting OCD.

Her eyes widened. "Why, that's the lace I added to the bottom of Julie's new shirt. Don't know why, just made her look bulkier and her with that nice new figure and all." The widow smoothed her hands over her own lace, as if to demonstrate how the absence of same would thin any figure.

Julie.

I remembered Dave's string of girlfriends, all fat—uh, pleasingly plump—okay, obese. Dave always complained about each fat girlfriend until she slimmed. And then she disappeared, to be replaced by another weight-challenged woman. Hmm ... a motive, but did slender Julie possess the means? And if she'd killed ol' Eagle Claw, how to prove it? She could always say that Mrs. McGarrity lied or that some other person, like me, planted the lace in Dave's hand, or that I'd never gotten it from Dave's body at all.

I gulped as I realized that with my thoughtless grabbing of the lace from Dave's hand, I'd destroyed any chance the lace could be used as evidence.

Unless Julie still wore that tucked in shirt, a shirt I suspected had a torn lace border. Maybe if confronted with the evidence of her crime—

Before I could get any further in my ruminations, there came a tentative knock at the door and Mallard's voice, "Mrs.

McGarrity could you please open the door? It's Mallard—I mean the police."

Mallard needed to work on his delivery. Although faced with Widow McGarrity, I might knock and speak softly. Especially if I believed she'd killed, she might kill again.

At the idea of innocent Mrs. McGarrity being accused and perhaps more, I plucked the only piece of evidence that could be used against her out of her hand and tucked it away. It'd be too ironic if my mistake somehow implicated the innocent widow. I pressed my finger against my lips in a "don't tell" gesture as Mallard knocked again, this time with more force.

Mrs. McGarrity raised her eyebrows but said nothing as she opened the door and confronted Mallard mid-knock. Dora, standing behind the sheriff, peered around his arm, right about at the level of his sweat stained armpit. I glared at Dora, who shrugged, hands out, palms up.

"I'm bringing you both in for questioning?" Mallard asked.

Mrs. McGarrity placed her hands on her hips. "Honey, that should be an order, not an order I'm going to follow, but you are the sheriff, remember?"

Mallard sighed. "Okay, then, how about this? If you don't both come with me now, I'll arrest you for obstruction of justice."

I transferred my glare to Mallard, and then blinked as I realized that Julie would be at the station as soon as she finished at Doc Byrne's. If I confronted her with the lace, maybe, just maybe—

"Better," Mrs. McGarrity said to Mallard, "but still not there yet. And I'm not coming—"

I grabbed her arm and earned a glare of my own. "Sure you are," I said, with what I suspected was a manic grin on my face.

Mrs. McGarrity's scowl deepened until it threatened to bisect her face. I widened my eyes and nodded, trying to convey via face contortion that I had a plan.

"What's the matter with your face, Tim?" Dora asked.

Mallard added, "Are you having some kind of a seizure from being guilty?"

I ignored both of them and said, "You and the other members of the Widows Brigade are always ready and willing to help out the cops, right?"

"We don't need help," Mallard said, probably recalling the other times the Widows Brigade "helped" the police.

"Hmmm," Mrs. McGarrity hummed, lips pressed tight.

Dora must have caught on to my psychic attempts to communicate, for she grasped Mrs. McGarrity's other arm and said, "C'mon, it'll be fun."

The widow's eyebrows raised so high they threatened to vanish into her grey hair, but still she complied.

Fun for unsuspected Dora, maybe, for me and the widow, not so much, but right at the moment all I wanted to do was thank Dora for her assistance in getting us to the sheriff's, where I could confront Julie.

* * *

"Doc Byrne called and confirmed," Mallard said to me from where I sat across from him at his small-for-being-sheriff desk, "that Dave—"

"Eagle Claw, he liked to be called Eagle Claw," I said. After some thought, I'd decided that Dave deserved to be called whatever he wanted, now that he couldn't tweak me about his Native American heritage. He couldn't bother anybody about anything, being dead.

Sheriff Mallard passed a hand over the sweat drops on his face. That man could sweat enough to water all our gardens. "Whatever, he was suffocated." Here Mallard made a horrifying gesture with knees raised and hands out, palms pressing against an imaginary zucchini, recreating the murderer's pose.

I grit my teeth and at sight of my face, the sheriff dropped his hands. "Mrs. McGarrity has arthritis in her knees and hands," he continued, "I don't think she could have killed Eagle Beak."

69

"Claw," I said automatically and earned a scowl from the sheriff. I sighed. Mallard seemed to think I was his primary suspect, maybe his only one. Certainly he'd planted me at his desk, giving Dora and Widow McGarrity each to State Police officers to interview in other rooms, so "the witnesses" wouldn't hear each other's statements.

"And if she couldn't kill him ..." Mallard trailed off, probably hoping I would break down and confess due to his rapier sharp logic.

How to delay until Julie arrived from Doc Byrne's? Maybe plant a zucchini seed of doubt in Mallard's mind about my guilt?

"I don't think Mrs. McGarrity could physically do it either but—"

"So what were you doing at her place?" Mallard jumped in and asked. "Planting evidence?"

More "showing evidence" but telling Mallard that might not help my case. I answered, but not his question. "But, I don't think you should limit your suspects to large people. Someone with a lot of upper body strength could have zucchini-smothered Dave."

Mallard leaned back in his ancient wooden swivel chair, which squeaked a loud protest. "Like who?"

"Like, um ..." How to frame my words so it didn't appear I wanted to frame Julie for my crime. And where was she? How long did it take to identify a body that we'd all already identified? Or was she doing something—

Julie walked into the tiny office, wending her way around the three desks crowding the space. Instead of wearing the same shirt, she now wore a tank top, to better show off her well-exercised arms, I figured. Just as I figured she'd run home to change. For an instant, a vision of Julie using those strong arms to press the huge squash over Dave's face flashed into my mind.

I swallowed a groan. My last hope of confronting Julie with the lacey evidence of her crime faded.

Maybe if I surprised her by yanking the lace out and waving it in her face, maybe she'd break down and confess. Maybe. Probably not, but it was worth an attempt to shift at

70

least some of the suspicion away from myself. I tried to think of a way to get her to come over to Mallard's desk. Wasted effort, for over she came, to stand next to my own squeaky chair and loom. It seemed to be a day for murder suspects looming over me.

"Why aren't you in a jail cell?" she asked in a tone that suggested I needed a trial, a judgment and hanging, and soon, maybe today. It looked like she'd decided the best way to protect herself from any accusations was to make a few of her own.

Why aren't you? I wanted to ask and swallowed the words. Still, I might as well try to deflect some suspicion. I reached into my pocket for the piece of lace, and my fingers grasped ... nothing. Another pocket, maybe? I rummaged around in my many, too many, pockets in my big men's cargo pants, avoiding Julie's gaze the whole while, not wanting to tip her off. My fingers finally found the scrap, just as I spotted something. Something better than any old piece of cloth.

Julie pointed at me and said to Mallard, "We found him standing over my boyfriend's body after killing him, why haven't you arrested him yet?"

"You mean you found me conveniently standing over him, a readymade suspect, after you killed him, left and then returned with Dora," I said. "You knew that the person that finds the body is always a suspect. You must have been awfully pleased to find me there."

Julie's mouth opened, but no words came out. She rubbed her eyes and sobbed. Yup, an act, and a good one, because Mallard stood and went to her, and then patted her shoulder.

"Whoa, hold up," he said. "You've got not a single bit of evidence against Julie here."

"I've got something better." I pointed down at Julie's pant cuff. "I've got a single zucchini seed, a huge one, so big that it had to have come from that squash on Dave's face."

Mallard left off patting Julie's shoulder and leaned down to stare at the thumb-sized seed. Julie's sobs increased.

71

I said over her faked distress, "You're the one who left and then came back. I'll bet if we ask Dora she'll say she found you close by Dave's. You never got near the body, so how'd you get that seed? You should have changed your pants along with your shirt, Julie."

With my last statement, Mallard straightened, took Julie's arm and said, "All good questions, you got some answers?"

Julie's sobs silenced in an instant. She drew herself up, showed her teeth and said, "I showed him, break up with me because I've gotten too skinny? I sat on him and squashed his face. Guess I hadn't lost too much weight living on this stupid zucchini after all."

As Julie confessed, Dora came out of the back room and stood and stared. When Julie finished, Dora said, "Well, that's one way to bean a guy—I mean zucchini him."

That's our Dora, always has the last word.

Sweet Dreams

When my husband rewired the house and I almost electrocuted myself I decided to kill him. My predicament's my own fault. I knew my husband was hooked on sleeper programs. I never knew it'd get this bad.

I met Henry when I clerked in a sleeper shop, one of the myriad ones that sprung up all over Boise, a tech-capitol and first adopter of the new technology. I made sure I was always the one to serve him. One thing led to another and we married. Now I know he married me because I knew a lot about the programs. I wish the fool things had never been invented.

I never bought a sleeper program before Henry and I'm never buying one after he's dead. Henry says they're the wonder of the western world—learn anything while you sleep. Put on a Swahili language tape at night and in the morning speak Swahili.

Except people, especially people like Henry, can't accept there's no real shortcuts in life. I told Henry that the subconscious level where sleep learning works is not long term memory retentive. Planned obsolescence. The programs fade away over two weeks. And they only work with a one-time application.

I told Henry that sleeper programs never create ability where there's none. Warnings printed on every package of S.P. tell a customer about potential problems. Henry never has read one of those.

There was the warning printed on the Olympic skier program Henry purchased for our winter vacation: "This program requires certain physical aptitude and agility to be effective."

I told Henry. He ignored me, took the program and his first time on skis hit the "Black Diamond" expert slope in Boise's nearby ski area Bogus Basin. Fine, if he'd had the body and co-ordination of an Olympic skier. Henry is fifty pounds overweight and falls over while putting his pants on in the morning. He broke a leg on his first, never finished, ski run and we spent our vacation money on hospital bills.

So what if the warnings are printed in a teensy font on the back of sleeper cassettes—you'd think he'd learn. Most people buy lots of programs at first, like any fad. Then they realize the programs don't change them into different people and then only buy a program for a real need. "Income Tax Preparation" is a steady seller before the April deadline.

This never happened to Henry. He never learns the limitations, never tires of the sleeper programs. He buys every new cassette. The cost doesn't deter my husband.

"Think of the money we'll save when I fix it myself," he always says to me. As if he knew one end of a screwdriver from the other.

Like when he "renovated" our kitchen. He "renovated" it back into the 19th Century and now I wash the dishes by hand and candlelight. Where was the money to pay a repairman? Spent on more sleeper programs. Instead of a dishwashing machine I get Henry speaking Swahili for two weeks.

I suspect he spoke it badly.

Then he insisted on taking an electrician's program to fix the lights. I found that he had fixed them by pulling them out of the walls and leaving live wires behind. I discovered that by grabbing one.

That's when I decided to kill him.

With no money left and our only assets a lot of used and useless sleeper programs, all that remains is the life insurance I took out on Henry. It's not as if I haven't given the marriage a chance, it's been six months. Six long months.

Also, it took me a couple of months to figure out how to kill Henry.

After all, I'm the first person the police will suspect. I had to discover a way that was foolproof and beyond question. And oddly enough, it was a sleeper program.

Working in the biz, I know some of its odd cracks and crannies, its shady side. I know who to ask for some of the more—um—unusual programs. Programs such as "How To Build An S/M Playground In Your Basement In Your Spare Time" and "Fifty Ways To Be A Drug Pusher" and other even stranger cassettes are available.

I've never told Henry about these programs, for fear he'll race out and buy and try them, until, while chatting with a co-worker, I found one I wanted him to try.

"Say," my fellow clerk said, with a giggle (she's sixteen), "have you heard about the latest nightmare?"

Nightmare is slang for the illegal cassettes.

"It's called 'How To Commit Suicide In Two Weeks Or Less Or Your Money Back.' What next?"

What indeed, I wondered as I purchased the program from someone who knew someone who was a sorta friend of somebody I kinda knew. Granted a suicide S.P. is not for your regular customer, but where there's a market ... and I'm not your regular customer.

When I got it home I steamed off the label from the outside of the package and glued on another label from a legitimate program I had also purchased, "How To Paper Train Your Puppy."

Henry's severely allergic to dogs, so I knew he couldn't resist such a program.

"Henry," I said to him over our candlelit dinner that night (with Henry's homemade-by-sleeper-program candles dripping dyed wax onto my grandmother's antique lace tablecloth, destroying it), "my old college alumni are having a class reunion next week in Portland. I know it's a bit of a drive and I'll have to stay with friends ..." I'd stay in a motel and I'd get no pleasure seeing the old losers from high school, but nobody knew that, including Henry.

Henry looked up from his beets. Beets grow well in Boise backyard gardens, unfortunately. We had home grown and canned, by Henry, until I almost died from a combination of food poisoning and the noxious weed he'd canned along with the beets.

He shrugged. "Sounds okay by me, hon. I'll be busy the next couple of weeks building the garage."

Another program—*hang yourself from one of the ceiling girders, please, Henry.*

"It doesn't matter if I take the car and drive?" I asked. Thank God Henry had not yet tried the car repair program so the car still ran. "I'd like to see the countryside—" I gulped at the huge lie. Much of the drive between Boise and Portland consisted of boring desert scrubland. "Sort of a vacation?" I added, hoping Henry didn't think about what I said. He almost never did.

"No problem," Henry said. Trouble was it was always a problem with oblivious Henry. "I know how you missed not having a winter vacation. Sorry about that."

Sorrier than you know, I almost said, but stopped myself in time. I said instead, "Oh great, I'll take a couple of weeks then, dear husband," and kissed him on his balding head. The "Grow Your Hair Back" program only worked on Henry's back hair.

So, after informing everybody I could think of about my wonderful vacation (my alibi vacation) I drove off to Portland. But first I left the S.P., gift wrapped, next to Henry's bed, a going away (forever for him) present. I knew he wouldn't wait to try my gift.

I drove to the reunion, every moment taking care to pay by credit card and chat up waiters and maids at the hotels. Then I attended the reunion. Every moment, I was bored to tears, which was excellent practice for me to be the grieving widow. Every moment I expected the call informing me of the tragic suicide of my husband.

No call came.

I took my time heading home, even staying overnight in Pendleton, town of blanket fame, along the way, although I could have made the drive in a long day. After all, the program did say two weeks. Or your money back.

Anyway, knowing Henry, it'd be several botched attempts before he managed to pull off his suicide.

But still, no call. So I ended up at home three days before the two weeks were up. Even as incompetent as Henry was, I figured he surely must have killed himself by now, even if by accident. Same difference.

With a great deal of confidence I drove into our driveway, gratified to see the building materials for the garage still scattered all over the lawn. No more projects! I walked into the house, expecting it empty.

Henry sat at the kitchen table, cleaning a gun. On the kitchen table sat a new S.P.: "How To Be A Sharpshooter."

Oh my. Was Henry practicing to not miss a really big, really close target, his head? I hoped so. But as I managed to get through the evening, I realized that save for the gun that he kept cleaning, Henry seemed the same old Henry.

Not suicidal.

After welcome home sex (my private parts never were the same after Henry used "How To Satisfy Any Woman"—ouch, ouch, ow) Henry fell fast asleep, the ear buds for "No More Snore" snug in his ears. His snores made the walls shake.

I pulled the covering label from the S.P., preparatory to replacing the original. I'd find the dealer tomorrow and get every dime of my money back. I checked the label to make certain it did say "satisfaction guaranteed" and boy, was I one dissatisfied customer. Then I saw what I'd missed. It was in tiny print, tucked away in one corner of the label.

"Warning," it said, "use of this sleeper program by persons not prepared to take final steps may result in extreme violent tendencies towards others in said persons."

That explains the gun.

In three days the programming on the suicide sleeper program runs out, so I only need to survive seventy-two hours. Seventy-two long hours. And with any luck, Henry will be as inept at shooting as he is at everything else. And I'm a moving target.

Just in case, I've bought a new S.P. for myself. I'm never interested in sleeper programs, but I might need this one.

It's titled "How to Survive a Bullet Wound."

Conda's note:

Here's a flash fiction piece inspired by my family's stories of Grandfather MacDonald, my great-great grandfather who came out on the Oregon Trail to Idaho. And while the final mystery will never be solved I have it on good authority, from my southern great-great grandfather's point of view, that he blamed all Yankees for … everything.

A shorter version of this story won second place in Hyde Park Books' Flash Fiction Relics, Fossils and Bones Contest, 2015.

Head Stands

Grandfather MacDonald broke his leg stumbling over a railroad tie while marching to the Battle of Gettysburg. He missed the battle. That set all right by him, for he was on the losing side.

"Better a bone crack than a rifle crack," he'd say, though the leg went bad and he wore wood below the knee forever after.

After the Civil War, he married a blind woman who had attended Ford's theater the night Lincoln died.

"Didn't see it," she said. "Course, I've never seen anything, don't know why that night'd be any different. I heard the shot though, a death knell, it were."

Together, the mismatched two came out to the Idaho Territory on the Oregon Trail. Grandfather MacDonald rode on the wagon all the way, his peg leg his reason. His wife always said there weren't no reason for him tying her, a blind woman, to the back of the wagon and making her walk, 'cept pure orneriness.

For five decades Grandpa MacDonald and his Yankee wife carried on a personal re-creation of the Civil War. "Pity Booth didn't keep on shooting," he'd say to her, "he might've got you."

He belonged to the South, so towards the end he gave ground.

His wife took to standing on her head, thinking it'd bring vision to her blind eyes.

Grandpa MacDonald, incited by the sight of his 75-year-old wife standing on her head, fled to the higher ground of the barn's roof, where he spent hours smoking cigars, in a temporary truce. Till the day he slipped on his wooden leg and tumbled off, broke his neck, and lived long enough to say, "I knew that Yankee'd get me some day."

We never did figure if he meant his wife or the soldier who shot him.

Conda's note:

This is a "prequel" short story to my Starke Dead *series. This story takes place when Starke was a dying mining town, high in the Idaho Rockies. None of the characters in this story re-appear in my* Starke Dead *novels. Hmm—yet!*

A Woman's Touch

Deputy Kelly Brown sucked in her lips as she studied the crime scene, worried that she might miss an important clue. The vast kitchen/dining space showed the aftereffects of a meticulous dinner and sloppy murder. Massive oak beams crisscrossed the dining room ceiling, framing the opulent wealth of a nineteenth century miner who struck a silver ore mother lode.

An attempt at tidying had been made, the table cleared and the expensive chef's knife jutting from the old man's chest wiped clean, but dirty dishes remained, stacked high in the double granite sinks. The maid had discovered the always mean and now dead old man this morning.

Kelly sighed. Who could tell how much evidence remained or had been destroyed? It figured that she'd get called out on her first murder on a case where clues, evidence and suspects abounded. It figured that it'd be a murder case in her first month as a new police officer, while she still worked to prove herself a real cop. It figured that she needed to prove herself to an old and old style Sheriff.

"Yup, it's a real mess," Sheriff Montgomery said. He pulled his heavy gun belt higher on his skinny hips. "Hoped you could turn a fresh eye to it, maybe add a woman's touch, being a domestic case—"

Kelly bit down on her lower lip to keep herself from backtalk. She reminded herself that the sheriff, almost to retirement age, had been the only law in the remote town of Starke, Idaho for decades. He wouldn't be living in the new women's lib world of 1972.

Still, he called her in, despite her newness, inexperience, and being a woman cop dumped into Starke, perhaps to get her to quit this man's world of policing. She frowned at her traitorous thought that since the dying mountain mining town's little crime was mostly on the level of Saturday night drunkenness, Sheriff Montgomery might be a mite inexperienced when it came to murder.

Her annoyance must have shown because the sheriff smoothed a hand over his regulation brown tie. His rumpled and stained tie, Kelly noticed with another twinge of irritation.

He said, "Why don't you interview the family members in their homes? They might relax and let something slip with your woman's tou—" He stopped and held out his hand toward her in supplication and apology. "Sure could use the help."

Kelly smiled at his attempt to mollify what he probably thought of as "her womanly feelings."

"Glad to help, Sheriff. Anyone you want me to start with?"

He shook his head. "Any one of 'em could be the killer. They all had plenty of reason."

One of them must be the killer, too. Comprised of four houses, plus two barns, built in 1879 on several acres, the family compound stood good twenty miles outside of Starke, up a long winding dirt road. No one had reported hearing any cars coming into the driveway that circled around the homes. Perhaps someone could hike over the mountainous countryside from the main highway, but the only possible suspects, those with motive, lived here.

Kelly considered the motive for killing the old man as she walked to the first log cabin of three surrounding the mansion.

From the maid's garbled tale, the old man had insisted his grown children occupy the much smaller cabins while he squatted in luxury in his vast house. He also insisted they attend his weekly dinner parties. The old guy loved to cook. This last dinner party, the maid had heard him announce he was

82

"disinheriting his ungrateful children and giving my millions to my favorite cooking school."

His two daughters and one son sat stunned through the rest of dinner and then hastily made their departure to their cabins to "mull over the news," as one of them had told the sheriff. One of them must have returned moments afterwards and stabbed the old man where he still sat at the table.

But who?

In the first cabin, Kelly met the oldest daughter, Marie.

Marie greeted her at the door wearing a formal silk cream pants suit. Kelly conducted the interview in a tiny sterile white living room, austere white carpet, gleaming drapes and furniture. The new deputy wondered if the decor was white to make the small room seem larger or if it only reflected Marie's chilly personality.

"When can we clean Father's place?" Marie asked again and again.

Kelly wondered why Marie seemed more concerned about the messy crime scene than her father's death. A touch of OCD perhaps? Or a way of deflecting her grief? She left Marie with more questions than answers. The woman had related the events of the previous evening in a bored monotone and said, "Dad changed his will like he changed his socks, with tri-daily frequency." A statement in direct opposition to the maid's account of the amazed siblings, so was Marie's tone a pretense?

At the next cabin, the door flung open to reveal the youngest daughter, Tammy, wearing stained sweats.

Kelly endured a few uncomfortable moments in Tammy's even smaller front room. Or perhaps it only seemed smaller, Kelly thought, as she shared a sofa with books, magazines, dirty clothing and old pizza boxes with the requisite empty beer bottles. Tammy sat across from her on an old ragged floor pillow and sobbed about her "dear old dad."

Ah, a more normal reaction here, but no confession or damning evidence to be found, unless growing loads of bacteria could be construed as a criminal offense. And like her sister, Tammy's emotional outburst could be an act.

Sighing, Kelly escaped, and with heart sinking down to her tired toes in their regulation, pug ugly boots, she knocked on the final cabin's door.

Here, the old man's son, Tom, bedecked in a clean apron, greeted her warmly with fresh baked, still warm, cinnamon rolls. Tom, who'd obviously inherited his father's cooking passion, (the myriad and well-organized cooking utensils crowding the pristine kitchen proved his love), plied her with the baked goods but no new information.

Like his sister, Marie, Tom appeared to be OCD about cleanliness, hovering over Kelly while she ate the roll and whisking the plate away as soon as she removed the last delicious crumb with her fingertip. Like his sister, he also talked of his father with a cold, clinical tone, a la "good riddance."

Headed back to the sheriff to report, in her mind Kelly reviewed the interviews. She slowed when she realized they'd told her little or nothing. Or had they? She stopped when she realized the suspects hadn't said anything that would lead to the killer, not a word, but they had shown her something new: how each lived at home.

Her heart much lighter, Kelly reported to the sheriff.

"Yes, I'm certain Tammy is the killer," she told the older cop.

"How could you know that?" the sheriff asked.

With a grin, she spread her hands and explained, "The killer attempted to clean up the crime scene, but still quite a bit of chaos and mess remained. Marie and Tom both inherited their father's clean-freakiness. No way would they have allowed a speck of food or gravy smear to exist after the murder."

To the sheriff's amazed open-mouthed look she added, "It just took a woman's touch."

Conda's note:

Now for a different kind of a "mystery" story, one about the crimes that family members sometimes do to each other, sometimes to the point of total destruction. This story was inspired by my family's events and history.

Walking with the Idaho Dead

The call came at night, as such calls so often do, and the policeman apologized for the lateness of the hour.

"Had to call, ma'am, I mean not that it's anything we can prove, you understand," the policeman, young by the cadence of his voice, hesitated.

"Yes? Is my grandmother dead then?"

"How'd you know?" he asked, the youth in his voice replaced by suspicion.

"She was ninety seven, what's the surprise?"

"Well ... the problem is, we're not positive she's dead. She's just ... gone."

"Gone? How can a 97-year-old woman with one bad leg, deaf and nearly blind be gone? Gone where?"

"Disappeared, not around, so far as we can tell." The policeman cleared his throat. "We suspect your uncle buried her."

I lay in my bed, the phone cradled in my hand, in the warmth beneath the covers, and thought of how mine is a family of long anger and no forgiving.

"We think maybe she died. But your uncle's not saying and since you're the only other surviving relative ..."

* * *

A day's travel later to Star, Idaho, I found myself smiling at a man that all my childhood I glimpsed only rarely. He stood

85

on the porch of my grandmother's house, his arms folded over his chest. Since I was five at our last meeting I feared he might not recognize me.

"Jane."

He knew me.

"Come into the house, I'll not turn a relative away, not like your father."

I remember grandmother always warning me, "Don't go near your Uncle Henry, child." In the back recesses of my mind, I still heard the echoes of his shouting that long ago day.

* * *

A hot sultry day in late September, the black walnut trees dropped their heavy load of nuts. We were all in the yard, gathering the nuts, hulling off the thick outer shells of skin and fiber that covered them. I tired of picking up the nuts and tried hulling them, but hated the sticky black fiber that stained my hands. So I stood, wanting to be helpful, as kids do, when my uncle yelled at my father.

They circled each other like dogs, my uncle screaming, my father silent. I ran to my grandmother and grabbed her apron. She pushed me away, not wanting the touch of my black sticky hands.

My uncle struck one blow, across my father's face that knocked my father down. "Get up!" my uncle shouted. My father sat on the walnut covered grass and stared at his brother until Uncle Henry turned and stormed into the house.

"A long time coming," my grandmother said, "but I'm not surprised."

* * *

Now, a quarter of a century later, I picked up my suitcase and followed my uncle inside my grandmother's house. A farmhouse of wood and plaster, built in 1913, it possessed only two bedrooms, the front parlor and the kitchen. Older than my grandmother, but not by many years, there was not one corner, one alcove, one chair or bed that did not retain some mark of her personality.

My uncle watched as I set down my suitcase and reacquainted myself with a house I thought of as a friend. In my high heels, I tottered over the wood of the front parlor floor. Uncle Henry watched my careful progress for a moment.

"I reckon I'll let you settle into it," he said, and banged out the door.

I took off my heels so I could wander.

The wood floors, long stripped of varnish, buckled with years of summer heat and winter cold. Hand-woven scatter rugs, with no rubber backing, lay over the more worn parts, adding to the impression that the floor was like a terrain of tiny hills and slippery valleys. I learned early to go barefoot and let the soles of my feet tell me the way.

Looking out the kitchen window, I gazed at the first telling signs of my grandmother's death. The back garden, always exuberant, lay ruined. Though the tomatoes, her pride, stood staked, they were but dry rustling stalks, wasted effort.

Every August, as a child, I had escaped the end-of-summer heat by sitting in the garden, the cool from the moist ground rising around me. Surrounded by the heady scent of ripe vegetables, I'd feast. The tomatoes, heated by the sun, would burst warm and sweet in my mouth.

Now I pressed my hand against the window, wishing the ruined garden to disappear, and when it did not, turned away.

As I joined Uncle Henry on the porch, a police car pulled into the dirt driveway. Three men got out, two carrying shovels. They stood next to the car, looking embarrassed. The third man, older, came up to the porch and introduced himself as the sheriff. He didn't waste his time with Uncle Henry but spoke to me.

"He tell you where he put her?"

I looked at my uncle. He stood rangy and lean, like beef jerky, all muscle and no fat, his knees locked back, legs braced apart, like he stood braced against a wind. My father, before disease bowed his legs, stood that way and the wind blew and never moved him an inch.

"Uncle Henry?" I tried to think of a way to get through to this man who long ago made himself a stranger. "Where's she gone?"

"Man's got a right to bury his dead," he said.

"That's true," said the sheriff, "but you can't just bury somebody without any preliminaries and in an unknown spot." The sheriff spread his hands, entreating reason from my uncle, whose reason fled years ago.

"Don't you want her to be buried with a proper funeral?" I asked.

Same as my father, Uncle Henry tilted his head to one side, his eyelids half down. "Why?" he said.

I shrugged at the sheriff, who signaled the two men with the shovels to come forward. They came, dragging the shovels.

The sheriff shrugged back at me. "Sometimes this happens, Miss," he said. "On account of there being these old family cemeteries around the old farmhouses. Aren't any new burials allowed because sometimes, with Star growing, the bodies just have to be moved. But they try to bury 'em—sentimental, you know. Is there a family plot on this land?"

"Not that I know of—" I looked over at my uncle. He'd turned his back. I didn't envy the officers their job, grandmother owned five acres, all that remained of the 2800 acre ranch my family once owned, and out behind the garden it was all overgrown, with an irrigation canal running through it.

The sheriff sighed. "Okay men, look for disturbed ground first." They moved toward the back.

"You take what you want from the house now," my uncle said. "I don't care what you take, but take it now." Uncle Henry followed the men.

As he walked away, I saw the slump in his shoulders. Grandmother must have been a heavy burden for him, for she was far from being a little old lady.

* * *

Over six feet tall, Dora Elizabeth Wylie towered over me even when I was grown. Raw boned, no one called her pretty, with her long horse face, but attractive with her grey eyes, that turned the length of her nose into an asset, the long face into an elegant counterpart to those eyes. She told me about an argument with my grandfather, a bitter fight that culminated in her asking why he ever married her.

"Figured if the mule died, you'd do to pull the plow," he answered.

First time she went out with a man, she went with my grandfather. She wouldn't have gone at all, being only fifteen; save that her older sister was sick and my grandmother went in her place.

My grandfather Harry took her to the dance in a sleigh that he borrowed for the occasion. Her fifteen years angered him. This grown man of twenty-five who muttered under his breath as he checked the horses' reins frightened Dora until he saw she shivered and he took up a bear rug and placed it around her, tucking it under her feet. They set off, through the early darkness of the winter night, with the bear skin tickling her nose.

At the dance all the other girls watched as she danced with him, this tall strong girl, homely save for her eyes, dancing with the handsomest man in the county. He danced most of the dances with her and she looked at the other girls and liked what she saw in their faces.

On the way back they shared the bear rug. He stopped the sleigh outside the fence that led onto her grandfather's ranch. It snowed light as feathers and she'd drawn the bearskin up around her face again. He looked out over the winter fields, saying nothing with her waiting, before he drew the bearskin down from her face and kissed her once.

Her older sister never forgave her.

Eight years later, Dora sat in the front parlor, seven months pregnant with her second son, waiting for them to come back from Harry's funeral. In seclusion, she sat in the front parlor with her swollen feet up and waited. Iris filled the parlor. She hated the sight and smell of it forever after.

At breakfast the day before, they argued. Harry sat at the kitchen table, his face grey in the early morning light.

She told him not to go to work on the rail line running from Meridian to Caldwell and then beyond, all the way to the Pacific. "They're dying on the line, dropping as they work, Harry, from that Spanish flu," she said.

"Have to, baby's coming, where we going to get the money?" he answered.

He left her sitting there. Two men carried him into the house later that day, unconscious from the moment he'd collapsed on the line. The doctor wouldn't let her near him.

"If I'd been able to see him, to touch him," she later said, "I would've made him stay, he wouldn't of left me then. But the doctor didn't want me having the flu that was killing so many, and me dying and the child in me, so they kept me away. Even so, he didn't die till the next morning. He waited for me to come and save him. They didn't even let me come and see him after he was dead and somebody, I don't know who, closed his eyes for him, not me. That ain't right."

Fifty years later, my grandmother did not attend my father's funeral either. "I don't approve of his being cremated, you should of asked me, I was his mother. It's wrong. I'm not going to watch some grotesque display of scattering his ashes."

* * *

Now, from around the corner of the house I saw the men moving out into the field, the sheriff and his men going first, Uncle Henry following. I went back into the house.

In the parlor I half expected the lingering scent of iris. I tried to decide what to take. Most should be left for Uncle Henry; he needed it more than I.

Stacked in the bookcase were old photograph albums. I sorted through several, remembering.

My grandmother never denied me my family's past. Every night I stayed with her, we lay together in the big bed, my head pillowed on her arm, her stories opening a window into her life.

But one story grandmother never told. She robbed a bank and took her son as a hostage, holding a gun to his head and threatening to kill him when the police surrounded the hideout.

90

Only five at the time my father remembered it all. How the police captured his mother. At the police station, having no place to put a 5-year-old, they locked him in the garage while they interrogated his mother.

My father never forgot huddling cold and hungry in one of the police cars. Above, in the station, he heard them yelling at his mother. He stared at a penny bubble gum machine all night long, but lacked a penny for a piece of gum to still his aching belly.

Grandmother spent two years in the Women's Prison, just outside the walls of the Idaho Penitentiary, while her young sons became too familiar with Boise's one orphanage. Every Sunday, my father and his brother Henry visited the prison, traveling in the back of an old wagon drawn by an obstreperous mule for the five miles between Boise and the prison. Although my dad picked long splinters from riding on the cracked and warped wagon boards, he loved those visits. The women inmates reached through the bars and stroked his chestnut curls saying, "Sweet little man, poor little man." He said it was the only loving he was ever to know as a child.

"That's why I didn't go crazy like my brother," he often said, "because I never knew what I missed, but before my dad died Henry knew about being a family."

For the deprivation of his childhood, my father never forgave my grandmother, until he ceased speaking to her altogether. As cancer raged through my father's body he turned away from any comfort she might give. She never forgave him this and told me about her recurrent dream.

"He comes on his birthday, he comes home," she said. "Always late at night, when I've been sleeping, he knocks on the door. He's got to knock, so's he can apologize, so's I can let him come home. I wake quick, move quick when I hear him knock, but I'm grown too old and when I get to the door, he's gone, lost again. I call, but he don't answer. Someday, someday, I'll get there on time."

I wonder if my father finally answered.

* * *

Now, setting aside the albums, I wandered out to the kitchen. Looking out the window, I saw the men returning from the back acres, one of them shaking his head, another glaring at my uncle. Standing there I remembered how my grandmother dreamt of my grandfather as well. He arrived for her in the sleigh and they went dancing, much as they had that first night. She awoke in the morning with the tickle of bear hairs about her nose. I knew then where grandmother must be buried.

I hesitated. Should I tell the sheriff and his men? Surely Uncle Henry had some reason for burying her there, in that manner. Or did he? Looking at my uncle standing stiff and silent, I wondered whether it was a final act of rage against his parent.

I stepped to the back porch and called out, "I know where she's buried."

Uncle Henry raised his hand, as if to stop me, maybe even strike me.

"You had no right, doing that, she's my family too," I said to him. I turned to the sheriff, "She's out at the old Star cemetery."

It took us longer than I figured to find the grave. One of the men spotted the fresh earth next to an old tombstone and called us over. The sheriff and his men left us, to go get the medical examiner.

My uncle and I stood, regarding each other over the fresh earth. The double headstone, with my grandfather on one side, and my grandmother's name and her real birth date already carved on the other side. Though the carving was done decades ago, the letters still stood clear. Someone had cleaned the stone and tended the plot, ringing the fresh earth round with marigolds, my grandmother's favorite flower.

"You're just like your father," Uncle Henry said, "never belonged to the family. Now they won't let her be buried here like she wanted. Guess this is about the only funeral she didn't miss. Didn't even get this one right."

Those were the last words my uncle ever spoke to me. He was wrong; she was buried next to my grandfather, after I renewed the plot lease and made all the proper arrangements. She had a proper funeral too, with a coffin and flowers, not iris, but I was the only one who came.

I would have liked to have a storybook ending, with my discovering a warm-hearted man in my uncle, hidden by the exigencies of fate. That we became friends and I found redemption in his likeness to my father. I wished that the family pattern might shift, somehow. I never saw Uncle Henry again.

I took the photo albums. Sometimes I stare at the old photos and then search my face for my grandmother's lineaments. Sometimes late at night, I wonder if a knock shall come. I will go and call her name.

I wonder if she will answer.

In my Starke Dead *cozy mystery series my main character, Dora, is a Buddhist. She's a Buddhist because I'm a sorta, kinda, semi-Buddhist. Or a person with Buddhist leanings who eats meat. Or something. My favorite thing about Buddhism is it's okay to be confused about Buddhism.*

Enjoy this riff on karma.

Bad Basenji Karma

An injustice and unjustified, I gotta tell ya—me coming back as a Basenji, the worst behaved of all the dog breeds. Sure, I used to beat up people, but that was my job. And didn't I get killed for refusing to break that old guy's legs? There was no reason for me to reincarnate as this horrid dog breed. How's a guy supposed to get a break, get on the path to something better than a Basenji, when I have to act like one? Almost anything would be an improvement. Pit bull, even.

And now I'm in jail. For doing nothing. Nothing. I stood on the kitchen table? Basenjis love high spots, my people know that. I didn't eat anything, not even the sugar out of the sugar bowl. Amazing restraint, but do they notice? Noooo ... they tried and convicted me and sentenced me to this horror.

I poke my pointy nose through the bars of my crate and sniff. The stew smells better than my once-favorite aroma, dollars in a cash wad of ill-gotten gains. My instincts kick in and I dig at the floor of the crate and whine, an eerie Basenji screech, before I force myself to stop. I gotta do better.

The bedroom door opens. Free at last. I've had an eternity, ten minutes, of cruel captivity.

A pair of pink-jeaned knees plunks down in front of the crate. "Barkly, Barkly," the three-year-old daughter, Debbie, cries in that so-annoying cute-little-girl voice. My people had a

Basenji before. They know the rule: "Basenjis: never with children." Jeez, I was never that dumb as a human.

And naming me Barkly? How gaggingly cute.

"Play, Barkly," the little girl says. She claps her pudgy hands.

Yeah, right, kid.

I squeeze into the corner. The little monster crawls in. I'm trapped. Maybe if I peed—nope, I gotta be good.

Gotta time my escape, or else—

"Barkly, dinner," the woman calls from the kitchen.

I shoot from the crate, claws scrabbling on the plastic. I'm not quick enough. The girl reaches and grabs my double-curled tail. And pulls.

Don't snap.

She tugs.

Don't snap.

She pulls harder.

Don't—I yelp and whirl around, jaws open.

I stop short. Whew, another karma strike adverted.

Giggling, Debbie releases my tail.

I bolt for the kitchen.

In the hallway, I pass a discarded used tissue. Tossed by Debbie, for the adults know the Basenji love for all paper products, especially used tissues. Yum.

I pause, one paw raised, drooling. Just one tissue? I shake my head. It'd be like an alcoholic with one drink. I'd be in the bathroom trash all night, eating paper products, being true to my base Basenji appetites.

Behind me, I hear the pitter-patter of three-year-old feet. Urgh. I sprint into the kitchen to my bowl and gobble. The kid sometimes joins me for dinner. Her parents think it's adorable when she "pretend eats" my kibbles. Yuck.

I finish and trot out to my favorite spot before the fireplace. It's part of my bad karma that my adoptive family lives where there's winter. Hey, I'm an ancient Egyptian breed, bred for the desert.

The living room, even with the fire, is freezing. I smell outside, strong and inviting. I follow the scent to the front entryway. The front door stands wide open. Since it's dinner time, everybody is rushing home. Car after car goes by.

Don't chase a car, becomes my mantra. I'm a sight hound. I chase. My legs quiver, but I force myself to stand. I won't give into my baser nature. Then I see her. Debbie. She must have opened the door. She heads toward the street.

"Daddy's coming home," she sings as she goes.

She's almost to the busy street with the tired, hurrying-home drivers who may not see a tiny toddler in the evening gloom.

I give a warning yodel, my first Basenji cry ever. I tear down the driveway and bump full body into Debbie just as she reaches the curb. She tumbles to her knees on the sidewalk and starts howling.

My momentum carries me forward. The last thing I see is a close up of a tire.

* * *

My eyes open. I'm in a box with other puppy bodies pressed close. I stare down a pointy nose. Oh no, I'm a Basenji again.

Sigh.

I force my eyes to focus on my brother next to me. He's fat and black with a long straight tail and floppy ears. Could it be? Am I a breed known to be gentle, good and well behaved?

Yes! I'm a Labrador!

Conda's note:

This short paranormal mystery story is the inspiration for my upcoming novel, Never Blink. *It's set in one of my favorite towns in Idaho, the capitol city of Boise, where I was born and now enjoy living and writing.*

Still Life

The word, "thief," spoken by my boss's wife, Jennie, echoed round the all-angles-knife-cutting-edges of the art gallery. My newest photo album slipped from my fingers to thump upon the knee banging low table. It fell right where I'd been about to sneak it into position while I cleaned. I'd arrived this evening a few minutes early so the staff of J&J Gallery wouldn't suspect it was me leaving the albums.

Oh no, my greatest fear—that I'd be caught in the act of placing my albums. Wait, no, couldn't be, Jennie had said "thief."

What was Jennie doing here? Although she was the owner's wife, Jennie almost never visited J&J Gallery. When she did, she made no secret of how the gallery took the precious time and attention of her decades older husband. I knew she meant away from her. I looked at the gorgeous young woman standing next to a square display pillar upon which was…nothing. On flanking pillars, two hideous matching statues of deathly gaunt naked women stood, enhancing the emptiness of the center pillar. Behind Jennie stood a police officer, shaven headed, his head the only thing rounded about his square muscular body.

"We caught you in the act, too," the cop said.

I glanced over my shoulder. The cop couldn't be talking to me. But no one, not a customer or even one of the gallery's two clerks, stood behind me. I always made sure I was invisible.

99

I always dressed in dark colored baggy sweats and made sure my dullard brown hair obscured my face. People forgot that I exist, which I adored. I made sure that they didn't first notice me, and if they did, they forgot the drab cleaning lady. I turned back to my accusers.

"I didn't steal this," I tried to say. The words flooded into my mouth and stopped, dammed by my teeth. I wasn't good with words, I was good with photos. If I spoke, I didn't want the next question to be asked, "If you didn't steal it, where did you get it?" A question I didn't want to answer.

"Ally didn't steal anything," my boss, Joe, stepped out of the stock room. I ducked my head at his destruction of my name, Albion. I'll take Al for short, but never Ally. That is, unless Joe called me that.

The rest of his harem, Marian, his senior clerk and ex-wife, and Libby, the other, much younger, clerk, followed right behind. Whenever I cleaned J&J Gallery, I struggled not to join those two adoring groupies. I worked to not adjust my drudge look, wear better clothes and tie back my hair. In his early sixties, Joe still retained his famous actor's good looks. But he'd never allowed his fame to destroy his good and generous nature. Instead, he'd parlayed it into his passions, an art gallery in his beloved "new hometown" of Boise, Idaho.

Marian stepped around Joe to point a French-nailed finger at my new work now resting on the table. "If Albion's not the thief, then what is she doing with the album?"

I worked as hard to not hate Marian as I did to not love Joe. Yes, without Marian's hard-natured and incisive eyes, the gallery would not have survived. Without her loyalty and service to her "best friend Joe," there wouldn't be the paltry money to hire me as a cleaning lady. Then I wouldn't have an opportunity to leave my "anonymous" albums, my art, my love, my life, in the gallery.

I chewed on a strand of my ragged hair. My album rested on the table, radiating my hope. Unlike my other albums of random, altered photos, my art photos, this album was crammed full with photoshopped pictures of a customer crowded gallery. The album would save the gallery, flood it with customers. Yes, it sounded nuts, even to me, but I believed my photos possessed the ability to shift reality. What an image showed became what was. It had happened before and I hoped it would happen again. If it helped Joe, it needed to happen.

New wife Jennie stared over at old wife Marian, amazement in her unlined face. It was rare the two wives agreed. Although Jennie shouldn't be surprised, they often agreed about anything around money matters, and theft was a matter of money lost.

"Al's the cleaning lady, she picked it up to clean," Libby said, her shyness making her voice lilt in a singsong. I recognized that lilt. My voice, the few times I spoke, possessed the same, with an overlay of rust. I looked over at my defender. She ducked her head, her mousy bland hair falling forward to cover her face. I knew that move too well, too. I winced as I wondered if Joe hired her and me out of charity.

Now, Libby stared through her curtain of hair, eyes wide and imploring, at Joe. She was a few years older than my twenty-eight, but around Joe she acted an annoying lovesick sixteen. I vowed to never act that vulnerable around anyone, ever.

"It's not Anony's album we're talking about," Jennie said.

I wished that nickname for the anonymous artist (me) had never been thought of, spoken or stuck.

"That's right," the policeman said. He stepped close to me and reached for my arm. I flinched away, not caring if it made me look guilty. I hated being touched.

The cop grabbed my arm. But his clutch was gentle, as if he feared I was as fragile as the gallery's art works. He may have been right; sometimes I feared I'd shatter.

"You need to come with me." He pulled a pair of handcuffs off his belt.

Images flashed through my mind, of the police officer vanishing in an overexposed photo, disappearing, his handcuffs with him.

"Those aren't necessary," Joe said.

"S.O.P," the cop said.

"Albion won't try to get away," Jennie added. "She's too frightened."

True, but I found it odd that Jennie, my accuser, expressed any concern for my state. Jennie, Joe's mid-life cliché trophy wife, treated me as moving furniture at best, an idiotic slave at worst.

Fear made me speak. "What proof do you have?"

"We have photographic proof," the police officer said.

My knees collapsed. *Oh no, no. Had they found my camera?* I'd secreted the small but powerful digital camera away, high in a vent. There it took a photo of the gallery floor every minute. When I retrieved the camera, I'd take the images and add customers to the often empty gallery. All to help Joe's flagging business flourish.

The cop held me upright and snapped on one handcuff bracelet, then the other. The sound cut into my spirit, sliced it apart.

* * *

"It's easy to manipulate images," I said, my anger making it hard not to sound patronizing. I rubbed one wrist with one hand and then switched to the other wrist.

After the uncomfortable trip to the police station, I found my knowledge of police procedure horridly expanded and my sympathy for accused innocents engaged. When we arrived at the ultra-utilitarian, cement block station, I guess the cop decided I wouldn't escape and took off the handcuffs.

"Especially electronic images," I added. *Which you as a cop should know*, I didn't add.

The cop, whose name was Brown, I'd found out on the trip over to the station, hit playback on the computer. Perhaps he figured showing me the tape over and over would get me to confess. I watched the cheap camera images jerk along the screen. A great many dropouts made the video run almost like a slide show. It showed a hideous sculpture of what appeared to be a naked anorexic woman on the square plinth, the matching women on their pedestals on either side, then a confusion of

102

images. A few grainy shots of me cleaning followed, and then more lost information. The tape ended with an image of me gone along with the skinny sculpture.

I grabbed the mouse and reversed the footage.

"Hey," Brown protested.

I paused the video between the footage of me cleaning and the end. "There," I pointed to the blur, "that could be a cut to another time, another day, after someone else stole the sculpture."

Brown leaned back in an office chair three sizes too small. "Why would anyone go to the trouble of doing that to security footage?"

I stared down at my tattered trainers. "I don't know."

I heard the cop sigh and raised my head. "I didn't even know things were being stolen," I defended myself.

Officer Brown looked at me as if I'd just confessed to bringing art into the gallery. "What did you think was happening to the stuff?"

"I thought the art was being sold," I answered. I bit my lower lip as it occurred to me that I should have known. J&J Gallery appeared too "California" for much of small-town-attitude Boise and sales were few and far between. I'd noticed things disappear, but had never suspected theft. It was too much for me, someone who leaves things, to imagine someone taking away those same things. I wondered if any of my albums had been stolen. I wondered what would happen to a thief who stole my albums. Nothing good.

At the officer's raised eyebrow I added, "I'm the cleaning lady, not a clerk, not in sales."

"Which, with your lowest pay rate gives you the biggest motivation for theft," Officer Brown countered.

I snorted, forgetting my fear and anger in the absurdity. I grabbed the computer mouse and ran the video back to the too-thin nudist. "And where does a cleaning lady sell something like this? At a yard sale?"

Where would anyone sell J&J's quirky art? I wondered. Unless the thief had no intention of selling the art—a glimmer of a suspicion flared in my mind. Remembered snatches of conversation strengthened it. I needed to get out of here and back to the gallery and get my camera from its hiding place. I needed to see what images I'd captured and what I could do with those images.

Officer Brown laughed, his face transforming to from cliché cop to friendly guy. I leaned back. I didn't want any friends. I wanted to be left alone to do my art.

"That's right, it's laughable my sister's a thief," my baby brother's voice came up from behind me. I hunched my shoulders. It'd been my hope to get out of this predicament before Adam found out. I hated what he'd think almost as much as what he'd say.

"And you are?" Officer Brown, back in full cop mode, asked.

"Adam Door, of *the* Doors of Old Boise," Adam replied.

"The Doors," Officer Brown echoed, but without the pompous inflection, "You mean, The Doors, that big honking house off Hill Road?"

Adam drew himself up to his full height of five foot five inches. "That's right, The Doors, built by one of the richest founding families of Boise." He laid a hand on my shoulder. "Us."

I twisted in my chair to look up at my brother. He stood with his skinny arms crossed over his thin chest. "Jeez, Adam, could you be any more portentous?" I asked.

Adam ignored me and said to Officer Brown, "So you might consider, Officer, that my sister has no monetary motivation for stealing."

I turned back to Officer Brown. "Sorry, my brother's about to take the Idaho bar. Guess he's practicing his pompous lawyer."

That earned me another chuckle from Officer Brown and a glare from Adam.

"Let's remember who's here under suspicion of theft," Adam said.

I should have kept my mouth shut, as I normally did. Being accused of theft had destroyed my usual pragmatic and reclusive self. I wanted to shout my innocence, but figured it'd be far better to catch the thief.

104

"I can't imagine you have enough evidence to charge my sister," Adam continued.

Frowning, Officer Brown turned back to his computer screen and played the video for a moment. He stopped "play" right at one of the jumps. "Maybe we don't."

Adam dropped his hand from my shoulder, no doubt surprised that the policeman agreed with him. Five years younger than me, Adam was more hard-headed and frozen into his opinions than I. A born attorney.

The officer gave me a hard stare. "Yet. So I'm letting you go. For now."

I didn't care that he sounded as if he read from the script of a bad TV show, I only cared that I was going to be free. Free to catch a thief. I sensed my brother shift back and knew he was taking a breath to pontificate again. I leapt up, grabbed Adam's arm and hustled him towards the door.

"Hey," he protested.

"When things are going your way, get going," I said.

* * *

"You'll be right back at the police station as soon as that cop runs a credit report on us," Adam said.

Not if I prove who the real thief is first, I'd almost blurted out. "Maybe, maybe not," I said instead. I focused on the curving, hilly road, driving the speed limit toward my home. Our home, rather, Adam's and mine, ours alone ever since Mom died five years ago. I could have driven the road with my headlights off and twenty miles above the speed limit, but didn't dare. Last thing I needed was a ticket.

"There's no maybe," Adam said. "We're broke. Unless you come out of the garden shed and let the world know you're Anony. And sell those albums instead of giving them away."

Ah, I'd wondered how long it would take Adam to start that ancient argument. I knew it wouldn't be more than a few minutes. And it wasn't. I strove to think of something different to say that would end the argument forever, or at least until I'd caught the thief.

As I turned into the open, elaborate, eight foot doors of a fence made only of tall, solid doors (ha, ha, very funny, great-great-grandad) I decided to say the simple truth. "Look, if you tell them I made the albums, I'll deny it. I'll say I stole them. And I'll go to jail and you'll lose The Doors."

We traveled in silence the rest of the way up the long oak tree-lined paean to avarice and arrived home. When I stopped the car in front of the massive wraparound porch, Adam jumped out of the car and strode to the huge house without a backward glance.

I sighed once and turned the car around and headed back to the gallery. The police had confiscated my key, but I hadn't mentioned my copy.

* * *

It should never be this easy. Even for me. My camera had come through for me, created what I needed. Again.

I flipped through the digital photos on my computer and watched my suspicions proved. I'd set the camera up to capture an image every sixty seconds during the gallery's open hours. That way, I'd be able to "layer" the few and far between customers until J&J was packed. Because of my setup, I'd caught a thief in the act.

I had to give her credit, Joe's wife, Jennie. She possessed a boldness I couldn't begin to muster, "stealing" items during open hours. Of course, Jennie was co-owner of the gallery, so she could have explained when she took the anorexic statue and walked out. Harder to explain would be her captured walking out with a security camera cassette a few moments after. I leaned back as Jennie's remembered complaints ran through my mind. *"You love this gallery more than me." "I want to travel, and not just to other galleries and trade shows." "I didn't quit Hollywood to come be an Idaho hick forever."* The thefts might be enough to destroy the gallery.

Questions crowded out the memories. Why had Jennie framed me for the thefts? Did she believe that Joe's misery over a trusted but dishonest employee would destroy his passion for his gallery? Or was it simpler than that? Did Joe suspect his wife so she had to find a fake thief? Who better than the nondescript, bit-of-nothing cleaning lady?

I twirled a hank of hair around my index finger so tight it hurt. This was all fine and great, but how to get the proof to the cops? If I took in the camera and the photos, there'd be nothing but questions. Questions I couldn't answer without outing myself as Anony. I could make an album and leave it in the gallery. But I could imagine Joe or Marian or even Libby putting the sudden appearance of such an album together with me and realizing I was Anony.

Even if I did confess to my secret artist life, what would prevent Officer Brown from insisting the photos were altered, same as the security camera images? I rubbed my hands over my tired eyes. There had to be a way. I looked past the computer screen into the clutter of my studio, searching for inspiration.

Adam called my studio a garden shed, but that was at best a mean-spirited misnomer. It'd been built as a small guesthouse back in the day when my family hosted lavish events, back before Adam's medical bills gobbled our wealth. The small house sported one large room with a tiny bathroom and kitchen—a place for people to change clothes, grab a snack or repair makeup, and rest, before foraying back out to an all night party. Now stacks of leather bound books, albums to be, lay scattered around the computer, as if tossed by a passing stranger.

Passing stranger. I sat up straight. Anony could be a passing stranger. If I created an album and then typed up a letter explaining that I, Anony, left the album at her home for cleaning lady Albion to find because I, Anony, had photos of the truth ... it might not work. But at least it would provide one layer of safety between me and discovery. Even if my photos had no power to shift reality, even if they were only bizarre manipulated images pasted into albums, I wanted to remain anonymous.

The album might not have to pass police inspection—if I convinced Joe and he confronted Jennie, she might crack. Worth a try.

I set about doing just that.

* * *

It took me all night, but by 9:30 a.m. I stood outside J&J Gallery, the new album tucked under my arm. I congratulated myself on striking the right balance in the album between telling the story I needed to tell and creating Anony's signature images. I'd even layered customers into several photos for luck. And with any luck, Joe would sell the album after I was cleared of the charge of thief. Sell it for a lot of money and turn the gallery's fortune around. All problems solved, via my special ability.

I stood straight for a second before remembering to do my downtrodden cleaning lady slump. Hopeful that Joe would be alone in the store, prepping for the 10 a.m. opening, I strode inside.

I stopped at the death displayed on the gallery floor. Jennie lay sprawled in a peculiar wax doll pose that whispered the truth that her life had fled. A halo of blood spread out around her head. Her eyes were slanted open, and for a crazy moment, I wanted to photograph those orbs to see if I could catch the killer in her last sight. That never worked. Next to her head, the anorexic lady statue lay, as if another murder victim.

Joe crouched on one knee next to the body of his wife, one hand reaching out, as if to shake her gently awake from a nap. Marian stood a few feet away, her purse on the floor, contents spilling. With one hand over her mouth, she resembled a lurid cover of a crime novel. Behind her hand, Marian's eyes shone with an odd, almost triumphant, light.

We might have stood frozen in our poses forever, save that Libby flung open the gallery door, raced inside calling out, "I brought donuts—" Then she saw Jennie's body, dropped the donut box in her arms, and started screaming.

Officer Brown gently took the album from my arms. With the thought that I handed him Joe's motive for murder, I let it go. We stood outside while an amazing amount of police officers and forensic people milled about inside the gallery. Joe stood with his head in his hands. Marian talked to another police officer. Libby sat in an ambulance, moaning, "He didn't do it," over and over.

I agreed with Libby, Joe couldn't have done it. Not for any reason. And he could simply have divorced Jennie. I remembered the strange look on Marian's face. I'd never quite believed her whole "we're-divorced-but-still-best-friends" bit. And it rang more false coupled with Marian's "Sure, I don't mind working as a clerk at my ex-husband's store while he lavishes money and attention on the new young wife." It seemed to me that Jennie's thieving provided a perfect opportunity for Marian to murder.

I studied Marian's expression while she talked to the policeman. Her face retained a smooth, calm veneer. She looked like someone describing coming upon a fender bender instead of a bloody scene of mayhem most foul.

"Joe didn't do it," I said to Officer Brown.

He ran a hand over his bald pate. "We'll see what the evidence says."

I knew what the evidence would say. Of course Joe's fingerprints were on the statue, it was his gallery, his stock. Of course, Joe loved his gallery with a greater passion than anything, perhaps even other people. And of course, the husband was always the prime suspect.

I closed my eyes and saw a photo of a different Joe, old, defeated, slumped on a cot in a cell. I opened my eyes to see Joe being handcuffed and read his rights. Myself an innocent accused, I knew a little of what he must feel as he was placed in the back of the police car. I couldn't, wouldn't, allow Joe's life to be destroyed.

I stared over at Marian and realized what I must try. I'd never done such an ambitious project before, but if it created a world with justice, it'd be worth everything.

It took longer than I expected. I had to go through hundreds of my images before I found the right ones. It took me four hours to alter the final photo to tell the damning story. When I finished, I'd transformed a photo of Marian placing a box on a shelf to one of Marian holding a skin and bones woman in her arms above her head—as if she were about to crash the sculpture down upon Jennie's head. To that one picture, I photoshopped in Marian frowning. She'd been looking at the gallery's recalcitrant cash register, but now she scowled at Jennie.

I stared at the image for long moments. I'd never attempted to manipulate a photo to tell a story from the past, only to present a possible future outcome. I shook my head. This wasn't Anony's work, this was only my pathetic and perhaps useless effort to show the truth. I placed the photo in a simple folder. I hoped it would be enough to save Joe and punish the real murderer, Marian.

I drove from my studio to the gallery in early night. Crime scene tape sealed J&J's front door. It was only a moment's work to cut through the tape. I stood, letting my eyes adjust to the darkness, then stepped forward and placed the photo on the now-empty-of-murder-victim spot. I turned to leave when all the lights flashed on.

Blinking, I stared at Libby standing a few feet away, a large gun in her small hand.

"Don't worry, Marian's not here," I reassured her.

"Oh, I'm not worried."

An image of Libby, statue held high, crawled across my mind. I swallowed hard and said, "You can put the gun down."

Instead Libby used it to gesture at the body spot where my file folder now rested on a smear of blood. "She deserved to die," she said. Her trembling lower lip told she lied. But if her lip shook, her gun held rock steady. "She was going to get Joe to close the gallery, one way or another. And then they'd go back to Hollywood and I'd never see Joe again."

As I looked at her, I saw the glints of mad obsession in her expression. Why had I never spotted that before? I considered myself an artist, with an artist's sharp eyes and piercing perceptions. How wrong I'd been. Or had I simply been unable to see in her eyes what might be in mine?

Libby focused the gun on the middle of my chest. "Now you need to die."

I wished I could alter audio the same way I changed photos. "Why?" I asked. "I only wanted to help Joe."

"You're the one who started all this."

"No, that was Jennie." *And she's dead now, so no problem,* I wanted to add but didn't dare.

"Without your albums, none of this would have happened."

The words "your albums" echoed in my ears. "I'm not Anony," I said, with all the force I could find behind those three simple words.

Libby snorted at my obvious lie. "*Your* albums were starting to bring buying customers in."

Even before I placed my customer-laden album? "They were?"

"Well enough so Jennie had to steal to get the gallery to fail."

I shook my head, trying to process the flood of revelations. "How long have you known Anony was me?"

"Always. It takes a loser to spot a loser."

Libby was right, my mistake in not spotting her had been one of degree. I didn't want to see more of what I hated in myself in Libby.

"But why kill me?" I asked again.

Libby sighed. "Simple. Joe's in jail."

Behind Libby, I saw Marian creeping forward. She must have snuck in while I focused on Libby and her gun. I forced my eyes to go back to Libby.

"When you turn up dead," Libby continued, "they'll know he didn't kill Jennie and they'll let him go and we'll be together."

Marian grabbed the closest skinny woman statue.

"No, don't," I cried.

Libby half-turned as Marian raised the statue high. For a millisecond, I saw my photo made real, not a past story but a present moment.

Then Marian brought the statue crashing down on Libby's head.

Before the police came, I snatched the now bloody photo off the floor. If Marian saw, she didn't say. She said nothing until Officer Brown gently took her outside, away from the blood and death.

After much questioning, the cops believed what happened and released us. Although Brown seemed angry and skeptical and told me he'd watch me closely. It helped that Libby still clutched her gun tight in her hand. Perhaps it helped that when Marian finally spoke, she kept saying over and over, "I only meant to stun her, make her drop the gun."

Now, I lie awake nights and tell myself it all worked out for everyone's advantage, except perhaps myself. The notoriety of the killings skyrocketed the customers coming into J&J Gallery, now renamed Joe's Gallery, providing success at last. Joe comforted Marian right into a re-marriage and both seem content. I told Adam about what I'd done with the photo and he hasn't mentioned selling the albums since. Best of all, no one knows I'm Anony.

Now, I lie awake and tell myself Jennie would never have been happy with her life, even if she and Joe had moved back to Hollywood. She wouldn't have enjoyed all the company of her older husband, much as she dreamt of that, as Joe would be miserable without his gallery.

Now, for long hours in the dark, I tell myself Libby's madness meant she'd be caught and caged forever. I tell myself she'd never want to live that way.

I hope if I tell myself over and over, someday I may believe my words.

Bonus Story

Plus Recipe!

Here is a story and my favorite recipe from my cookbook Starke Deadly Delicious, *a cookbook based on my* Starke Dead *mystery series—with real recipes! A couple of caveats of my recipes are that they are all fast and easy to make, plus delicious.*

Mama Chin's Live Forever Casserole

Mad Maddie Starke stared down at her menu and frowned in her signature facial expression of pure fury. She stared up at Mama Chin, whose calm gaze didn't waver a micro inch. Mama Chin knew all about Maddie's blow and bluster.

Maddie pointed at a word on the daily special on Mama Chin's Save On Café's menu. "What the heck is that?"

"It's quinoa," Mama Chin said, resisting the overwhelming urge to sigh. She couldn't resist a shift from aching foot to aching foot. She needed new wait staff. It didn't work anymore for only her and Paul to try to run the café all on their own. Not with the ski resort successful.

"Keenwah? How do you get that from quinoa? Why isn't it qwe-noah? Like it's spelled?"

"I agree totally."

Maddie's eyebrows raised high at Mama Chin's agreeing with her, which almost never happened.

"But, we've got to update our menu to sell to our new customer base, you know, the health-nutty skiers?"

Maddie's eyebrows remained halfway up her forehead. "Do you think I'm a health nut?"

Mama Chin regarded her friend; remembering how Maddie's favorite meals were meatloaf with gravy, chicken pot pie and bacon and eggs. "Not really."

"Don't you have a real food daily special? You know, meatloaf with gravy? Chicken pot pie? Bacon and eggs?"

Now Mama Chin sighed. "No. You can, however, order any of those at the regular price."

Maddie reared back in her chair. "How many generations have our families known each other? Have the Starkes ever ordered off the regular menu? It's a matter of pride—"

Mama Chin leaned forward to stop Maddie's word flood. "And have any of you ever had a bad meal at the Save On Café?"

Maddie wrinkled her brow. "Well, once Great-Grandpa—"

"I can toss any customer out of here, you know."

Maddie glared. "Okay, okay, I'll have the quinoa casserole."

* * *

Maddie patted her mouth and then her tummy.

"Well, how was it?" Mama Chin asked.

"I'm so glad I'm always open to new experiences, especially in the realm of good food." Maddie gave her mouth another prim and somehow smug pat. "And that I've decided to eat more healthy."

Mama Chin crossed her arms over her chest. "First time for everything. So does that mean you'll tip for the first time?"

Maddie's shocked expression was her answer.

Quinoa Casserole

Since the quinoa in this recipe gets baked in the oven, it doesn't need to be precooked. Instead, it settles into the bottom of the pan and creates the casserole's crust.

INGREDIENTS:

- 1 teaspoon butter, margarine, olive oil or coconut oil
- 1/2 cup uncooked quinoa
- 8 eggs
- 1 1/4 cup milk or soy, almond or coconut milk (the coconut milk is good with curry spice, instead of the other spices, for an "Indian" Egg Bake)
- 1 tablespoon chopped garlic
- 1 teaspoon chopped thyme (optional)
- 1 teaspoon sage (optional)
- 1/2 teaspoon salt
- 1/2 teaspoon pepper (or more if you love pepper)
- 2 cups packed baby spinach, roughly chopped (or you can use frozen spinach, thawed and squeezed dry, as well)

—OR—

- 2 cups of the vegetables of your choice, green beans, corn, peas, cooked carrots, or a combo all work well. Note: this is a forgiving recipe, but the texture will be a little too chewy if you leave out the vegetables.
- 1 cup finely shredded Romano or Parmesan cheese or any hard cheese of your choice (may be omitted, but casserole will be a little bland, more like an omelet). Fake cheese, such as soy cheese, doesn't work well as it tends to not melt and burn.

DIRECTIONS:

Preheat oven to 350°F. Grease an 8-inch x 8-inch glass or metal baking dish with butter; set aside.

Put quinoa into a fine mesh strainer and rinse under cold running water until water runs clear, then drain well. (Note: If you don't rinse the quinoa well, it may be a touch bitter. It also sometimes contains fine grit. Run your fingers through the seeds as you rinse.)

In a large bowl, whisk together eggs, milk, the spices you've chosen, and quinoa. Stir in spinach or other vegetables then pour mixture into prepared dish. Cover tightly with foil then jiggle dish gently from side to side so that quinoa settles on the bottom in an even layer. Bake until just set, about 45 minutes. Remove foil and sprinkle top evenly with cheese. Return to oven and bake, uncovered, until golden brown and crisp, 10 to 15 minutes more. Set aside to let cool briefly, then slice and serve.

VARIATIONS:

Try different combos of spices and see what you like the best. Me, I always splash in a little hot sauce because I love hot sauce! I also add a couple of tablespoons of nutritious yeast for an even cheesier taste.

Also, this makes a good "corn casserole" side dish if you just use corn as the vegetable.

Just for fun, here's a cautionary flash story to end my anthology Mild West Mysteries: 13 Idaho Tales of Murder and Mayhem. *You might recognize a request within.*

Ending: Reader's Choice

Dora pointed at the dead woman's body slumped forward at her desk, her forehead resting on the keyboard. "I bet I know what she died of," Dora said, annoyingly answering my unspoken question.

I sighed and worked hard to tell myself that I loved being the sheriff of Starke, Idaho. Sometimes. Not right now. I rested my hand on my holster, the leather already a bit sweaty from my touch. "What are you doing here?" I asked Dora.

"Nothing. I just, um, dropped by to welcome her to Starke and found ..." Dora's chin dropped to her chest. "Oh Buddha, I hate how I keep finding dead people."

"Yup, you've got a real talent," I said and snapped my mouth shut. Where'd that yup come from? I'd better watch it or I'd be a clichéd western sheriff, chewing tobacco, wearing cowboy boots and drawling, yuck. Time to be a regular cop.

"What do you mean you know what she died from?" I asked the one other living person in the room, Dora. Narrowing my eyes, I studied the body. No signs of violence, unless a spilled mug of coffee, the mug emblazoned with "Writers Do It with Words, counted.

"Did you kill her?" It seemed reasonable that's why Dora would know why the writer died. Although she didn't have a single motive to murder her new neighbor that I knew of—yet.

"Me?" Dora pressed a hand to her heavy cotton, wax spattered apron. "No—I mean—well—maybe—I should have, um ..."

I reached for my handcuffs at the back of my belt. Taking Dora to the station might clear her speech.

Dora must have spotted my reach, for she blurted out, "The author died from a lack of reviews of her books."

"What?"

She pointed at the computer screen, where the author's Amazon title page endlessly refreshed itself. "See? No reviews."

Ah. Now that I thought about it, I'd heard of the "review lack death phenomenon." An author's life blood is the reviews they receive for their books. Without reviews, an author can wither, collapse and die.

"I read her book and was going to leave a review, but I forgot," Dora said. "So I'm partly to blame for her death." She hung her head.

Reaching out, I gently patted my friend on her shoulder. "I'm guilty too. I read her book and never got around to reviewing it."

Dora lifted her chin. "From now on, I swear to review the books I read."

I nodded, vowing to go home and review the book I'd just read. After, of course, I called the coroner, supervised the crime scene specialists, filled out the paperwork, got dinner, walked the dog and …

(And this living author thanks you for your honest review.)

Read on for the first chapter of *Starke Naked Dead* the first in my *Starke Dead* cozy mystery series. Next up: *Starke Raving Dead*, to be followed by *Starke Howling Dead*. Can you tell I'm having fun with titles? Here's a brief blurb:

The gossiping women of the Widows Brigade in the new ski resort of Starke, Idaho love a good scandal—this time it's a murder mystery, and a stark naked corpse!

Jeweler Dora Starke believes creating her own jewelry line with no money and no time is her biggest problem. She's mistaken. When her recluse dad shows up and thrusts a stolen, cursed jewelry piece worth millions at her and demands she sell it or he's dead, she knows this must be her biggest problem. She's wrong. When she pursues her father to his Idaho mountain cabin and instead of dear old dad, discovers a stark naked corpse, she's certain she's found her biggest problem— whodunit. Nope. Dora's problems are just beginning...follow Dora as she becomes an amateur sleuth to solve the mysteries of cursed jewelry and murder, in this, the first of the Starke Dead *humorous cozy mystery series.*

Starke Naked Dead, the first chapter

The bell rang. My father, Wild Rupert the mountain recluse, shuffled inside, his shoulders hunched for a blow. I jumped up from my stool behind the checkout counter.

"Dora, I'm in trouble," Rupert whispered low and hoarse. His wet lower lip wagged and displayed the rotten stumps of his bottom teeth. A sweet stench of decay wafted my way.

First time in months I'd seen my father. He never ventured into Mad Maddie's Marvels, my aunt's store. He never dared.

Yet he stood in front of me. Backlit by the late afternoon sun streaming through the front door of Mad Maddie's Marvels, his long grey beard trailed around his shoulders.

He crept a few steps inside. "You have to help me."

A deep warmth spread in my chest. First time my father ever asked me for anything. "I'll help you, Father. Anything. I'll do anything."

Rupert slid his hand into a pocket of his ragged leather duster. Strips from the lining of the old coat hung to the floor. It gave off a faint aroma of old tanned hide, nasty, vile, but familiar and thus, comforting.

He dragged out a jeweler's velvet bag, the largest made. Covered in soot, the filthy bag once had been a deep burgundy, the color of old blood. My father loosened the drawstring and withdrew a grimy blue flannel rag.

I clutched my favorite Ohm pin, a backward three with a couple of dashed accents, which rested on my jeweler's apron. I watched, transfixed.

He opened the first corner of the rag. Silver flashed in a stray sunbeam.

"Oh, what have you got?" I breathed.

He unwrapped the rest and held out the rag on his open palm, a sacrificial offering. There, on his calloused and acid-scarred hand lay a necklace.

I gasped, grasping my Ohm pin so tight it cut into my palm.

Twelve two-inch heart-shaped cabochon blood rubies, each nestled in a platinum heart setting, created the heavy collar of the necklace. A pendant of a naked woman carved in onyx and set in platinum depended from the twelve links. Worth millions.

"Sell it." Rupert thrust the rag with its valuable burden toward me.

Unbidden, my hand reached toward the necklace. The enormous piece glistened with platinum and rubies and black onyx. Oh, my.

The necklace flowed balanced over his hand, resplendent on the dark blue flannel rag. The voluptuous woman pendant hung from his fingertips. Perfect. No, not perfect. Torn solder dangled from one tiny foot, obscene.

I wanted to pin the necklace to the glass counter and grasp all that glory. I jammed my hands into the encyclopedia-sized pockets of my jeweler's apron.

"Take it, quick," my father said. His voice quavered, his beard trembled. "Before Maddie gets back."

I started. We both glanced around the store. If my Aunt Maddie returned and found her despised brother-in-law here we faced a storm of mad Maddie trouble.

"Who's the designer?" I demanded.

I wanted, no, needed to know. The elements of the necklace screamed Art Nouveau. The design glowed unique, the work of a master jeweler. But I couldn't place the necklace in an oeuvre. "Vever?"

"Sell it," Rupert said.

"Lalique?" I knew as I said it, the necklace couldn't be a Lalique. In everything, including his jewelry, he always used glass. Onyx, a dyed semi-precious stone, didn't count.

"Sell it."

"A Verdura?" I asked, before my father's words at last sunk in. My head jerked up. I stared at Rupert. "What do you mean, sell it?"

He gave the rag bundle a shake. "Now. Today."

My mouth hung open. "B-but, where, where did you get it?"

Even at the height of his popularity and fame, when he was renowned all over the West for his "Starke" designs, Rupert never enjoyed the resources to create such a piece. I doubted any designer did today. Platinum went for well over a thousand a troy ounce.

My father shook his head. His fringe of long grey hair flew. "If you love me you won't ask any questions."

"No questions? You've got to be kid—if I love you?"

First time he spoke of my love for him. And he used it like a club.

He looked far worse than when I'd seen him last. His clothes, always old and worn, but always clean, were grey with grime. His spirit, blue.

I gulped back bile. Good thing I'd not eaten in hours. It was tough being a vegan in Starke, Idaho.

"I've run out of time," Rupert said. He spoke to the floor. "Sell it today."

"Today?" I glanced around at Aunt Maddie's shop, at decades of dust and disorder. I couldn't sell the Crown Jewels in this mess. I imagined the shelf with the potato salt-and-pepper shakers, priced at three dollars a pair, and next to them the necklace. Worth millions.

"Get cash, no checks." Rupert's hands shook as he clutched the bag and the necklace with its soiled flannel.

"Cash?" I rubbed my face in disbelief. "Cash?" Nobody had that kind of cash, not even the wealthy who would flood into Starke as soon as its ski resort opened in two weeks. Buddha willing and the snow should fly.

Rupert stuffed the necklace back into the dirty velvet bag. "Take it." He held out the bag, his hand shaking.

I took a step back and bumped into the display case of spud-based souvenirs. The case rocked. A little Spuddy Buddy fell off onto the floor and produced a poof of stale dust. "What? Where did you get it? Where did you find it?"

Where could my father have found such a treasure?

"I need—at least a—a hundred thousand."

"A hundred thousand?" My voice squeaked. "Dollars?"

"It's worth millions. Even a bit damaged—even with a bit missing." He fingered the bag in his hand, a talisman. "And it's worthless." His chin dropped to his chest. "To me," he whispered.

"But who would have a hundred thousand?" Even as I spoke I realized I knew one person with tons of money. She might know who created the necklace as well. She knew everything. Or so she always insisted.

"Your boss," Rupert said. He knew too.

"Nance is not my boss. Not any more. Not ever again," I said. "Now I'm my own boss." I refrained from another chaos check of the room.

"She's rich."

"Yes, but I'll bet she doesn't have a hundred thousand stashed in that battered steamer trunk she carries around as a purse." Although, I believed the cash might fit into Nance's voluminous satchel.

Rupert gulped. "Dora, please, I've never asked you for anything."

And you've never given me anything either, I wanted to blurt out. Ohm, I breathed. As a practicing Buddhist, and boy did I need a lot of practice, I knew that a brutal accusation would so be not Right Speech.

"What are you going to do with a hundred thousand dollars?" I couldn't imagine why Rupert needed all that money. He never needed money before. He lived in a tiny cabin in the woods. He sold a few of his "junk" jewelry pins every fall to buy food for the winter. His clothing he got from the Widows Brigade during their annual "Charity Party."

"No questions. I have to have the money. Now. Today."

The slanting afternoon light through the dirty front window grew dimmer. "Today is gone. I can't—"

"You have to," Rupert insisted.

124

"No, we have to tell Lester," I said.

Lester the Arrester, Starke's Sheriff for thirty years, would know what to do. He always knew what to do. Or had known, before.

"No, no, no." Rupert placed the bag next to his heart. "Promise you won't tell." He looked over his shoulder at the front door as if checking an escape route and then back at me. He shook his head. His never-shorn beard waved from side to side. "If you tell anyone," he shook harder, "or if you don't get the money now, I-I'm—dead."

"Dead?" I threw my hand out to steady myself. The display case toppled over.

Rupert and I jumped as potato-shaped salt-and-pepper shakers, butter dishes and flower vases all with "Souvenir from Idaho" scrawled across them in flaking gold paint crashed and broke.

"Maddie will be mad," Rupert said, his voice high, threaded with fear. He glanced behind him at the front door, as if he feared she would appear at the speaking of her name.

"Wait. No problem and good riddance." I didn't want him to run before I had some answers.

Rupert stared at me. "But your aunt…"

I flapped my hand at the broken junk, dismissing it. "I'll take the blame. I don't want the tacky things in Maddie's new improved store." Aunt Maddie's renovated store would showcase my original jewelry designs.

The corroded bell above the door clanged. Another thing I'd replace. A blast of frigid air followed the bell. Too cold to snow, darn it.

A woman's voice sang out "Hello?"

The necklace flashed as Rupert stuffed it back in the velvet bag. "Get me the money. Or I'm dead," he hissed. With a desperate nod he tossed the bag to me.

I caught it on the fly and thrust the bag into my apron pocket. Even in my oversized jeweler's apron, the bag bulged the pocket. Ugh.

I couldn't see the woman behind my tall father. I peeked around him to where she stood in the doorway. I stared at an even-shorter-than-short-me plump figure. Unfamiliar. The woman's long thick golden hair cascaded past her waist and obscured her features.

"Pardon me, please, if you don't mind," the woman said in a high, childlike voice.

Rupert flung his hands up and froze, a terrified statue.

"It's not Maddie," I reassured him.

I wondered how many years it'd been since he and Aunt Maddie spoke. Although my father should know that my aunt would never begin a sentence with "pardon me." She might not even say "please." And she never cared if anybody minded.

Rupert looked over his shoulder. He gasped.

The woman looked up at him. "Is it—could it be?" She flung aside her curtain of hair. Her large blue eyes widened. "Bertie?"

End of Chapter One

Conda V. Douglas

Award winning author Conda grew up in the ski resort of Sun Valley, Idaho. Her childhood was filled with authors and artists and other creative types. She grew up with goats in the kitchen, buffalo bones in the living room and rocks in the bathtub. Now her life is filled with her cat and dog and permanent boyfriend and writing.

She's traveled the world from Singapore to Russia (in winter!) and her own tiny office, writing all the while. She delights in writing her cozy Starke Dead creative woman mystery series with amateur detective jeweler Dora Starke. The more Dora discovers cursed jewelry, her aunt digging graves, and a rampant poisoner, the more fun Conda has—although sometimes Dora complains about her plight! The first in the series, *Starke Naked Dead*, won Third Place in Mystery in the

Idaho Author Awards 2014. Next up, *Starke Raving Dead*, in which Dora's mad Aunt Maddie proves the aptness of her name.

When she's not writing Dora into her quirky and quixotic mysteries, Conda writes the popular tween fantasy *Mall Fairies* series. The fairy inspiration for her *Mall Fairies* came from the sparrows that live in the Boise Towne Square Mall in Boise, Idaho. When not rescuing fairies from humans, cats and themselves, Conda works on the last title in the *Mall Fairy* trilogy, The *Mall Fairies: Destiny*.

Learn more about Conda here:

Blog: http://condascreativecenter.blogspot.com
Twitter: https://twitter.com/Conda_V
Amazon author page: https://www.amazon.com/author/condadouglas

www.ingramcontent.com/pod-product-compliance
Lightning Source LLC
Chambersburg PA
CBHW071351170626
46811CB00003B/1100